QUANTUM PHYSICS & MY DOG BOB

stories

PAT RUSHIN

BURROW PRESS | ORLANDO, FL

Published by Burrow Press
PO Box 533709
Orlando, FL 32853
burrowpress.com

First Edition.
© Pat Rushin, 2017. All rights reserved.
Book Design: Vero Stewart & Liesl Swogger
Cover Photo: AVID Creative

ISBN: 978-1-941681-81-7
eISBN: 978-1-941681-82-4
LCCN: 2016945592

Distributed by Itasca Books
orders@itascabooks.com

The author expresses gratitude to the following publications for their faith
in originally printing the stories in this collection: *The American Literary
Review*, "Vow"; *The Southeast Review*, "This Is Just to, Like, Clue You"; *The
North Atlantic Review*, "Every Goddamn Thing"; *Lake Effect*, "Quantum
Physics & My Dog Bob"; *Black Rock & Sage*, "Terrible Secret" (now titled
"The Garden"); *Zoetrope: All-Story Extra*, "Call"; *Provo Canyon Review*,
"Dig"; *The Tonopah Review*, "Spider Rock."

Burrow Press is supported in part by its subscribers, members, and:

About the Author

PAT RUSHIN is the award-winning author of *The Call*, a novel, and the story collection *Puzzling Through the News*. His original feature-length screenplay, *The Zero Theorem*, was produced in 2014 by The Zanuck Company and Voltage Pictures, and directed by Terry Gilliam. He has published essays, screenplays, poetry, but mostly stories in a variety of literary magazines, including *Zoetrope*, *The North American Review*, *Quarterly West*, *Sudden Fiction*, *Indiana Review*, *American Literary Review*, and elsewhere. He teaches creative writing at the University of Central Florida, where he has also (twice upon a time) served as editor of *The Florida Review*.

Also by Pat Rushin

The Call: a virtual parable

Puzzling Through the News

For Lacy & Bonnie, my inspirations

VOW

a prolix parable

The man hadn't slept well that night, and at dawn he was already up and dressed. He opened his bedroom window to the winter air, startling a flock of cackling grackles from the branches of his backyard oak. His wife, still snugly quilted in bed, murmured a cranky protest at the draft. "Shut it," she complained, and at that moment, though he'd be hard pressed to articulate why, the man decided to cease speaking for the rest of his life.

At first, no one seemed to notice. He sat lost in thought behind his newspaper as his children bickered over breakfast, their mother threatening them no less than three times with revocation of television privileges before they shoved each other out the door to catch the school bus. She looked to the heavens and swore. "Why do I bother?" she said. "And *you're* certainly no help." The man pursed his lips and exhaled heavily, as if to say: "I can tell them precisely nothing that will change their lives. (And it's best, by the way, as I've mentioned many times before, not to harangue them with punitive strictures you don't intend to follow up on.)"

At work that morning, he nodded at his colleagues in the hallways and settled himself quietly in his office. Almost immediately, his project manager appeared in the doorway, curtly reminding him of the report that had been due on her desk first thing this morning. The man bit his lower lip, shuffled together the scattered pages of yesterday's draft, and wagged his head wearily as if to say, "The world whirls about me at an ever quickening pace, but I'll finish it PDQ and have it for you ASAP. (Mea culpa, BTW.)" After she'd gone, he scrutinized the draft. He'd planned on revising again, cutting it back, clarifying it, refining it. Instead, he carried his report to the copy machine and stood idly duplicating page after page of thoughts whose germs could only prove fruitful through multiplication. When he placed the required number of copies on her desk, the man's project manager bristled slightly, though apparently not because he'd delivered the document without a word.

"It's about time," she said.

•

There's a limit to how long a person can remain silent in this world before arousing curiosity and concern, and soon enough, the man was required by both family and employer to seek counseling.

In the interest of streamlining therapeutic inquiry, the man spent a full day preparing a written explanation of his behavior. ("On My Silence" he entitled the single-paragraph abstract, the last words, as it happened, that he would ever write.) In brief, the statement professed that he suffered from no mysterious mental disturbances. He'd simply gotten to a point where he couldn't stand hearing the sound of his own voice. The hemming and hawing, the holding forth, the repeated explanations, remonstrations, reiterations: all were for nothing. Hadn't the world heard enough from him to date to last it the rest of his relatively brief life? Really, he hadn't anything of importance to add to what he'd already said countless times, to what others had already said countless times before him. Everything he'd ever had to say now struck him as tautologically tedious. His voice, he insisted, had come to display all the gravity and import of a fart chasing the wind. He was through wasting his breath.

"I'm all talked out," he penned in conclusion. "Enough said."

A lengthy line-up of psychologists and psychiatrists lateraled his case, one to the next, each dumbfounded by his apparent obstinacy. The man hadn't always been easy to live with, his wife informed each new therapist. Their marriage had seen its share of disagreements, especially once the kids came. *So many of them so soon!* he used to complain, as if he'd had nothing to do with bringing them into this world. Once upon a time, they'd argued regularly, and he'd certainly been at no loss for words back *then*. He'd fire salvos of wounding words late at night when the children were in bed, words that once or twice had her on the verge of filing for divorce. But she attributed their former troubles to his drinking, something he'd given up years ago (cold turkey, just like he quit smoking, one day at a time without the benefit of a 12-step program). No, aside from the occasional (and perfectly normal!) hissy-tiff of no great consequence, he'd been a model husband.

Until he clammed up.

Psychologist and psychiatrist alike puzzled over his case, some prescribing years of analysis, others opting for the quick fix of anti-depressants, several suggesting a rigorous course of operant-response conditioning, and one diehard insisting that a healthy dose of electro-convulsive therapy would have the man jabbering like a monkey in no time. The man proved himself to be a pleasant if uncooperative subject (listening attentively to all of the questions he refused to answer and keenly inspecting all of the tests he refused to take), and, eventually, all of his therapists confessed themselves stumped, stymied by the man's stubborn refusal to yield them a single syllable of speech. Still, the man seemed otherwise sane and certainly posed no danger to himself or others. Despite his blatantly passive-aggressive idiosyncrasy, the man should be capable of leading a relatively normal (if socially and professionally disabled) life.

Given the man's (relatively) clean bill of mental health and faced with the decision of placing him on disability, his project manager (in a brilliant stroke, if she did say so) had him transferred to another department. His new duties took him to a floor full of cubicles that held dozens of quiet employees independently involved in making sense of long and seemingly senseless columns of numerals and esoteric mathematical symbols. Many of his colleagues wore personal CD players and headphones to work. The man followed suit, and soon he could not be distinguished from his fellows.

•

Time passed, and the man and his family settled back into their normal routines. At first his children conspired to goad him into speaking. "Dad?" one would say, "I'm pregnant." "Have you seen my crack pipe, Daddy?" another would try. But the man only smiled and shook his head, and soon enough they let him be, making room for him on the sofa during Friday night movies and passing him the popcorn without him having to ask. In time, his children turned solicitous of his silence, speaking in hushed voices around him, affording him a semi-reverent respect he'd never elicited with reasoned lecture nor top-of-the-lung tirade. His youngest, barely old enough to speak herself when her father cast off his yoke of words, took on the role of spokesperson for him, generously forgiving certain failings of his that, heretofore, his children had righteously railed against. "That's just Dad's way," she'd explain to her siblings when he somehow, unremarkably, betrayed their expectations. If she caught him frowning in speechless disapproval, "What Dad's trying to tell us," she'd interpret, "is we should give his poor ears a break!" But if the older children sometimes grew nostalgic for the long-gone sound of their father's voice (reading *Goodnight, Moon*, say, or *Now We Are Six* by the soft glow of a bedside lamp), they had to admit that he maintained an inexhaustibly pleasant demeanor, now that he'd silenced himself. All of his children felt free to share their problems with him. He'd listen patiently, brightly compassionate, and, when the rendition was finished, lay a hand on the child's shoulder as if to say, "I, too, was once young and uncertain of my place in this world, but things have a way of working themselves out. (And if money can help, I'm at your service!)"

The man's wife, of course, had a more difficult time adjusting. Initially inferring his silence to be a veiled criticism of her naturally chatty disposition, she countered with a grumbling, cold-shouldered silent treatment of her own. When that tactic didn't serve to loosen his tongue, her restrained resentment often boiled to a lid-popping tizzy. "Talk, you selfish son of a bitch!" she'd hiss. "Open your mouth and say something!" She coaxed and pleaded, threatened and cursed, all to no avail. Finally, she gave up on him and (for the first time in a long time) once again considered divorce. But his quiet tears of desperation (supplemented by the repeated pantomime of pointing to his eye, his heart, and then to her) softened her resolve. He loved her, it was true, and if he wasn't able to tell her that in so many words, the soft moans deep in his throat while they made love, the semaphores of his hands flagging secret messages across her flesh spoke volumes. He showed his love in countless ways, from helping out around the house without complaint to surprising her with flowers and jewelry (gifts easy enough to point to through a glass showcase). What more could a woman want from a man? What more was there to say? Over time, she became accustomed to his silence, though she occasionally missed the rumble of his baritone crooning pop love songs, the tickling whisper of sweet nonsense in her ear late at night after the children were in bed.

·

Before long, the man's children were grown and gone, returning on visits to deposit their own darlings for Grandpa, beaming brightly, to dandle on his knee. Soon, even the man's children's children had grown too old to cuddle, and their infant gurglings and nonsense syllables evolved into whimsical rhetoric as intricately pointless as a game of chess. They could yackety-yak the livelong day about nothing at all! The world had come to seem like a call-in talk show on the radio, the gist of which the man could follow in a disinterested manner without feeling obliged to join the debate. He was on the same frequency—he listened, he understood, he even empathized— but he was wired as a receiver, not a transmitter. Which was just as well, for the more he listened, the more he became convinced that, despite the ubiquitous chatter in this world, no one seemed to hear anything anyone had to say anyway. His thoughts remained unremarkable, but they were all his own. No need to share something the world had an abundance of.

But as his allotted time in this world drew closer and closer to closure, the man sometimes caught himself trying to recall the last words he had ever spoken, as if those words were somehow important. *Words*, he thought. *Birds. Fright. Flight. Sing.* It had been so long now. At first, he dimly recalled, he'd felt the temptation to speak daily, more so than anyone could imagine, but he'd always fought the urge. He was used to fighting urges (one day at a time). Once, lying in bed beside his wife, unable to sleep, he'd reached for her, touched her, and at that moment nearly let his heart pour out a torrent of tormented testament (the subject of which he couldn't for the life of him imagine now), but he'd restrained himself. A single word, he knew, would be his downfall. *Words. Birds. Light. Sight. Sing*, he thought. His final words didn't matter, he supposed. Whatever they'd been, they weren't worth preserving: no call to etch them on his tombstone. They were words, just words— used up, played out long before he'd been born.

One evening, he lay in a hospital bed, his wavering vital signs chirping like crickets in the dusk. His wife sat at his bedside, humming the melody to some long lost torch song, life's sweet and salty lullaby echoing in his ear. A spasm shook him: the chirps grew frenzied. A hand squeezed his tightly, fingers nervous as starlings, and he opened his eyes.

"Are you all right?" his wife said.

His mouth was unbearably dry. He gestured toward the water pitcher on the bedside table.

His wife touched the pitcher, raised her eyebrows. "What's the magic word?"

The man smiled. He pointed to his eye, his heart, and then to her, but the well-worn pidgin pantomime failed to satisfy her.

"I'm serious," she said. "Say something. Anything." Her eyes glistened. "Don't leave me without a word."

Dark wings clouded his vision, and suddenly a thought occurred to him. It was a new thought, it seemed, one he couldn't recall ever thinking before in all his days of sunrise and twilight, one that he would take to his grave unless he spoke it now. He swallowed. He worked a creaking rumble from deep inside his atrophied larynx. His lips trembled, and his wife leaned close, closer, heart teetering with desperate hope. "Say it," she pleaded. "Say it!"

And so the man opened his mouth and cleared his throat one last time. He sobbed with effort, wondering for the first time in a long time at the best way to put what he had to say, at the proper way of phrasing his final breath in this age-old world of unspoken promise. *Please*, he thought. But the sudden chirping deafened him, and the cool light of awe took his breath away.

"Oh," he managed, and then he died.

Aside from that solitary exclamation, the man left only his legacy of everlasting silence. In time, his widow recovered from her grief and remarried. Her new husband, a retired man of the world, filled her ears with endless renditions of his storied past. This was a man who just wouldn't shut up. He droned on and on in a humdrum nasal monotone day after day about God knows what.

And oh! How she hearkened in dumbstruck delight! His voice was a gong, a wonder beyond words.

THIS IS JUST TO, LIKE, CLUE YOU

"I have eaten the plums..."
— WILLIAM CARLOS WILLIAMS

So you ate the nectarines that were in my half of the refrigerator's bottom crisper drawer and which you knew, you *knew* I was saving for breakfast, since I'd clearly informed you from the start (to be answered by your raised eyebrows and sudden laughter) that my macrobiotic diet prescribed daily doses of certain fruits and fibers that weren't always easy to obtain.

"You and that dweebly diet," you snickered. "I'll order you a lentil pizza, call it even. Hey, you got any milk besides this acidophilus? I put some in my coffee yesterday, and I'm like parked on the can all morning. How can you *stomach* it, Sissy?"

Clue: My name is not Sissy.

When I reminded you that the lease sharing agreement we signed the day I answered your ad three months ago promised mutual respect for private property (along with separate fridge and pantry shelves), you rolled your eyes.

"You're not like the only roomie I interviewed, Sissy-kins. You're just like the boringest. If you don't like it here," you said, deploying dramatically low-throated chuckle, "then move."

Which I'd considered daily since night two with you, when you brought home your "youngbloodstud *de nuit*," as you drunkenly called him, and treated me to hours of dramatic howlings from the other side of my bedroom wall. "Just another night in paradise," you glibly assured me the following morning after you'd whisked your lover out the door with a belly-full of my bran flakes for his breakfast. "Lighten up, Sissy-doll."

But moving was no option, given the reasonable rent and my shoestring finances. My planned Ph.D. in English did not come cheaply, not with me paying full tuition from my father's meager life insurance policy, with no prospect (my first year, at least) of the fee-waiver and stipend your M.F.A. program had bequeathed its premier and already-published hotshot young poet.

"Originality pays," you'd calculated before our first week together was through. "That's why I gave up the lit-crit shit. I'm creating something new, not vulturing the canon's marrowless bones. Hey," you'd said, pulling weathered leather notebook from hip pocket, "I can use that."

Still, you chose to eat my nectarines, and, adding insolence to injustice, felt inspired to return the fruitless pits to their plastic produce bag, appending to it a purple post-it note emblazoned with your infantile, unrhymed, unrhythmed, plagiarized "poem" telling me how "way cool delicious" they were. When confronted with your trespass that morning, you smirked and, in lieu of apologia, said simply: "I don't explain my poems."

"*Your* poem?" I said.

Dark brows arched beneath ragged blond bangs. "My version, anyway, thanks and a tip o' the hat to Bill C. Williams."

"I'd still like an explanation."

"I don't explain his poems either."

"You ate my fruit," I persisted. "Not the two or three I'd gladly have shared if you'd asked, but all six of them."

"Oh, yeah, like you'd share. And it was seven, I think."

I ignored your barb. "Did you stop to think I might like some? How could you eat *all* of them?"

"Wasn't easy," you said, standing before the bathroom mirror, applying too much black eyeliner as usual. For someone so strategically aware of her physical arsenal—lithe legs lengthened by baby-doll skirt, lissome neck sturdied by crew-collared halter—you displayed a tactical blind spot from the chin up, masking your plain but pretty face in near mime-quality blacks and whites. Your choice of scent, too, was all wrong, a darkly muscular musk more suitable to a linebacker than the former high-school gymnast you claimed to be. "Truth is, I only ate four," you continued. "Hank ate the rest."

"Hank?"

"Or Jake. Or Hal, maybe. The guy I brought home last night. You were already in bed, thank God. Hank's short for Henry, right? Hal's short for Harold? Harry? Probably Hal," you mused, oblivious to (or perhaps purposely provoking) my growing impatience, "'cause he sure was hairy. Wasn't short for anything, though, if you know what I mean, and you probably don't. That's your problem, Sissy-doll. Not enough sex. Are you getting any at all?"

I held my temper. "Why would you and Hank or Jake or Hal or Henry or whomever deliberately set out to eat—"

"That's *whoever*, Sis. Don't go grammatically anal on me."

"Deliberately," I repeated, "eat all of my nectarines?"

"Jesus, Sissy, chill." You combed fingers through spiked

dye-job. "Think of it as performance art, a dramatized found poem, a rejuvenated aesthetic statement."

This gave me pause.

"Plus I was high, and I was hungry." You rubbed your taut belly above low-slung belt, your navel ring, which had always unnerved me, glinting between your fingers. "I, like, couldn't resist. Sweet Sissy's forbidden fruit, so fresh and juicy…" You winked, licked the full length of your middle finger from palm to black-lacquered nail. "Mmm-mm good."

In retrospect, I realize now, it was then that I first felt it: the stab of pain in my own belly, anger's piercing antigen. At the time, I thought it a simple twinge of PMS, imaginary inner child's muffled kick to ovary, hastening flow of egg's unfertile woe. That or heartburn. A spoon of baking soda in a glass of warm water should do the trick, I thought.

"Why," I said evenly, "must you always be so cruel?"

You showed surprise for a moment, then quickly recovered. "'Cause I'm a poet," you countered. "And poets tell the truth. And real truth hurts."

"What truth are you supposedly telling me?"

"Whatever truth there is, Sissy."

"My name," I told you, as you well knew, "is not Sissy."

"I like Sissy better," you shrugged. "It suits you."

•

"So is she a dyke or what?" my boyfriend said that evening.

I'd been dating Kyle for five weeks, and the one time I'd dared bring him to our apartment, you teased him mercilessly, probably because he was a neatly-groomed MBA candidate instead of one of your usual unkempt louts, your brooding brutes, your anemically sociopathic aesthetes.

"Are you guys, like, getting it on?" you had the indelicacy

to ask him, laughing loudly at his blushing demurral. Worse yet, you kept insisting he have a drink, even after he explained that his diabetes precluded all alcohol. "Come on, one won't kill you. Loosen up, Carl."

"It's Kyle," Kyle said.

"Jerk-off," you said after he'd left. "Loser-city, Sis."

Now, in Kyle's apartment, sitting side-by-side on the sofa with him, his lean, khakied thigh touching mine, I frowned. "I don't see what her sexual orientation has to do with anything," I said, "but no. She's hetero. Promiscuously so."

"Bet she's bi, at least. Anyway, time to get even. Eat something of hers, why don't you?" He smiled in a lascivious manner I didn't care for. "Food, I'm talking."

"I'm on a fairly strict diet."

"Then we're just going to have to kill her, I guess."

"I have poisoned the plums?" I joked gamely.

"Over my head, but I got the perfect poison." Kyle was a voracious reader of mysteries, believing that a plot that didn't spring from and/or lead to murder was no plot at all. "Some night when she comes home high—alone—we wait till she passes out and shoot her up with a syringe or three of my insulin. She goes into shock, checks out, and it looks like an overdose or alcohol poisoning or whatever."

"Wouldn't an autopsy show the insulin?"

Kyle scratched his flat-top. "Dunno. I'd have to check. Do they autopsy everybody who ODs?"

I refrained from telling him that an autopsy was never performed on my mother, who died, strictly speaking, of a self-administered IV overdrip of morphine (her thumb punching the button again and again as my father and I discreetly turned our heads) though the death certificate listed lymphoma by way of breast cancer as cause. Two years earlier, the autopsy performed on my Spartan older brother verified what incredulous ICU doctors already suspected: my only sibling, unaided, had checked into ER in the final stages of untreated (and by then untreatable) melanoma. No autopsy had been necessary for my father, the last to go and the one to last the longest. He'd managed the pain of pancreatic cancer all through my Master's degree, hobbling his way to my commencement ceremony with newly-implanted bile shunt already necrotizing the surrounding flesh, finally succumbing at home, where he chose to be, his hand in mine.

"What have I done to you?" he rasped before gratefully gasping his last. "What have I left you, my love?"

Aside from the modest term policy (barely enough to bury him and bankroll my first year toward the doctorate), only his professed undying love—that and a list of prophylactic dicta cached (along with unpaid medical bills) in a safety deposit box and addressed to me in his hand. Entitled *Things to Avoid*, my father's hard-learned legacy included, in order:

- All power lines & microwave ovens
- Sunlight (even wearing so-called "sun screens")
- Smoking & smokers (tobacco or otherwise)
- All chemical solvents (esp. those commonly found in ordinary household cleaning products)
- All intrauterine contraceptive devices (e.g. loops, coils, copper 7s) as well as insertable sponges & tampons
- Anything grilled over charcoal

But that was between me and mine, not for Kyle's ears (and certainly not for *yours*, till now), so, instead, "Only when they suspect foul play," I answered. "But be serious. I don't know how to handle her."

"Everybody has roommate problems sooner or later."

"Thanks for the input."

"Hey," he said, stroking my hair. "You okay?"

"It's the stress," I sighed, feeling it metastasizing the more I thought of you. "She's the rudest, most insensitive person I've ever met. She plays obnoxious music when I'm trying to study, leaves her things lying all over, brings home all these awful men, criticizes my clothes, my eating habits, my opinions. She wrote a poem comparing my—" I stopped, voice rising, fought for breath. "My vagina," I managed, "to a *clam*."

You remember your masterpiece, darling roomie, don't you?

clamped tight beneath night's

sea of sand, urchined to no

avail, languishing in

depthless despair

of ever being

levered

open

Which you had the audacity not only to present to *me* but to your workshop's critically pitiless eyes as well. "They butchered me," you complained. "They raped my poor pussy poem. Last time I anthropomolluskize *your* precious cherrystone, Sissy-kid."

"Um," Kyle said. "What's she know about your vagina?"

"What do you mean by that?"

"Hey, I'm not implying," he said. "Don't infer I'm implying. I'm just, you know, *ask*ing."

"Let's just forget it," I said.

"Dyke," Kyle decided, rising. "Dick-tolerant vagitarian all the way. You want my advice? Do what she says. Move."

"I can't afford to."

He knelt before me, touched my knee beneath skirt's hem. "You can if you move in with me," he said, voice earnest, hand inching upward. "I wouldn't even charge you rent."

And oh, how I suddenly wanted to! How I wanted to flee your amused cruelty. But I'd only known Kyle a few weeks, and, though I thought myself capable of falling in love with him eventually (his eager humor and wiry optimism reminded me of my poor lost brother's), I'd kept a rein on our passions thus far, hearkening (only posthumously, it's true) to my mother's long-unheeded advice to save myself for someone I loved and respected, someone who loved and respected me in return. "A good man," she'd said. "A man like your father."

So far, Kyle had been patient, if bemused and sometimes frustrated. "I respect you," he'd said just last night when I drew the line in his car after the movie, "but you can't be sure of love till *after*." He referred to our romantic attentions as "Petting Lite" and let me know that although he admired my refreshingly old-fashioned position on sex, he hoped to change that position soon enough, come which time he'd be eager to accommodate whatever new position I chose.

"It's too soon," I told him now.

"You wouldn't have to sleep with me."

I moved his hand from my thigh, laced my fingers in his.

"Your body, yourself," he said, clearly deflated. Then, "Hey," he said, "what's your secret?"

"I don't have a secret."

"Everybody has a secret. Tell me yours. That's what lovers do, tell each other secrets. Humor me. Pretend we're lovers. Tell me a secret."

"What kind of secret?"

He looked away. "Like you weren't molested when you were a kid or anything, were you?"

I let go his hand.

"Not to be nosy, but a guy has to wonder."

I thought of my father and brother, their gentle ways reduced to tabloid formula, both gone now, leaving me alone and loveless in a senselessly insinuating world. I frowned.

"Not at all," I answered, finally. "Quite the contrary."

•

When I returned to our apartment, you were busy primping for another night of bar-hopping. Whenever *did* you write?

"Want to come with?" you offered, walking from your bedroom. You adjusted the last in a glittering column of ear studs that encircled both lobes. "You could get lucky."

Though only two or three years my junior, you had the uncanny power to make me feel ancient. "Thanks," I said. "I have a paper to finish."

"I figured." You tugged at your thrift-shop tuxedo vest, further exposing the cream of your bra-less breasts. "That Emily Dicklesson thingie, right?"

"Dickinson, yes," I said. "How did you know?"

"I saw it on your desk," you said.

"You were in my room?"

"Just browsing. No big deal. Jesus, Sissy, are you actually going to turn that thing in?"

"I can't believe you invaded my privacy."

"That's because you're so antisocial. Old Emily's the perfect poet for you. Talk about low-estrogen verse!" And here you began to sing "I like to see it lap the Miles" to the tune of "The Yellow Rose of Texas."

"Stop," I said.

"How would your department's reigning theorists put it? You're privileging what a dead white male academy expected from a female poet. Em heard a Fly buzz—*dash*—when she died. You gotta love that flaky feminine punctuation. Because she could not get a life—there's that adorably imprecise dash again—Death kindly stopped for her." You laughed scathingly. "Safe and quirky abstractions, dreamy death wish pabulum. Ain't that just like a woman? Let me clue you, Sis. In *today's* academy, if you want to write about Dickinson, you'd better prove all her poems were about the secret abortion she had after getting it on with her minister. That or out her as a closet lesbian. As is, your Ph.D. and a week's worth of sucking off the chair'll get you an adjunct job teaching five sections of bonehead comp. Don't forget to swallow."

I stood aghast, the pain suddenly clarifying itself as ovarian. How fitting. I could feel the ripening mutation with pin-point accuracy now, stabbing me near speechless.

"Why?" I managed.

"Why what, Sissy-dear?"

"Why are you telling me this?"

You smiled sweetly, lips glossed corpuscle red. "Because I like you, silly. I wouldn't tell you anything if I didn't like you. How come you never tell *me* anything?"

"Such as?"

"Such as *anything*." You turned for the door. "Never mind."

"What if I told you *your* poetry sucks?" I taunted. "How would you like that?"

You stopped, faced me. "That'd be a start, but you wouldn't be telling me anything I don't already know. You think I'm not in the same boat? You think I won't have to suck miles of cock to get some tenure-trackless community college gig?"

"You're published," I offered, defensive.

"Right," you said bitterly. "That's what got me this cush fellowship at Podunk U. Published all of five poems, two legits in the undergrad litrag, two questionables in my faculty advisor's pompous poetic journal. Only had to sleep with him twice before he printed them. Only had to smile at his wife once at a faculty-student happy hour before I didn't have to sleep with him ever again. I haven't published anything since. Haven't written anything worth a damn since you moved in, if you want to know the truth."

"You slept with your professor to get published?"

"Oh, Jesus, Sissy, grow up. I slept with my professor because he turned me on. I didn't plan to prostitute myself for publication. If going to bed with him earned me a better read, that was a bonus. And don't look so ethically challenged, Miss Prim and Prissy. You don't know how many times I've wished I *hadn't* slept with him, just so I'd know if my stuff was *really* any good." Your eyes moistened for a moment, then hardened cavalierly. "But the way things are going now, if there was anybody with clout in this program, I'd be straddling his lap before you could say *New Yorker*. A fuck is just a fuck," you purred, "but a published poem is forever."

"Lord," I breathed, shaking my head. "Do you even realize how callous you sound?"

You toyed with the doorknob, preoccupied. Then, "Take my advice," you said. "Find a fresh angle for that paper. That or find a dissertation committee you can go down on. And good luck," you called over your shoulder, closing the door behind you. "Faculty here's a bunch of eunuchs. Male *and* female."

•

After you left, I turned to my Dickinson paper. How unfair, how *wrong* you'd been in your assessment of her. Her work had been startlingly original, unconventional, *dangerous* even, in the context of nineteenth-century letters, and she'd been only grudgingly admitted to the canon. How could you so arrogantly dismiss an entire life's work? Though it wasn't due for another week, I'd planned to polish the paper that night, perhaps obtain my professor's preview of it the following day in order to incorporate whatever suggestions he might have. I pictured myself in his office, my paper propped in his lap between us, me leaning forward studiously, his gaze dropping southward toward my negligently-buttoned blouse. Our knees touch, and he fingers his beard, intrigued by a particularly astute insight.

And then I felt it again, sharp and undeniable, the rampant growth gone awry, cells mutating, dividing, amassing, outwitting the T-cells in the guard tower by deftly masquerading as eccentric citizens to cover the armed uprising. This was the way it started. Cancer needn't breach defense's walls. It scaled those walls from inside and perched on a parapet of subconscious, flinging fibril, fibril, fibril (thanks and op. cit. to W. Whitman) to enrapture and capture my very soul.

I would need an oncologist soon enough—that or a shrink—unless I chose to accept my family's legacy without a fight. For now, though, I could not bear to suffer alone.

I penned a hasty post-it note to you—"Gone to K's"—and walked the arbored shadows cross-campus to his apartment. I rang the buzzer again and again before he finally answered the door, sweatpantsed and shirtless, breathless and bleary-eyed. I hugged him around his bare waist. He drew back, distracted.

"Were you sleeping?"

"I must've dozed off," he said, face flushed.

"Can I stay here tonight?"

"Sure," he said, rather nervously, I thought. "I'll sleep on the sofa."

I followed him to his room where, broad back facing me, he brusquely brushed and straightened rumpled sheets.

"You don't have to do that," I said.

He fished a wad of Kleenex from between the sheets, crumpled it in his fist. "Good thing you woke me," he said, picking up a pillow and plumping it. "I fell asleep without taking my insulin. Want to get my kit from the medicine cabinet?"

As I turned toward the bathroom, I caught sight of him quickly pulling something from beneath the other pillow, heard his nightstand drawer open and close. When I returned, he was sitting on his bed, initial discomfort replaced by a slow smile.

"Want to help?" he said, opening the kit, and, at his gentle urging, I sat beside him, watched him (for the first time!) as he tested his blood sugar. I winced at the swift jab of lance to fingertip, the blood welling brightly. *This blood*, I thought, this *pure untreasoned flow*, and at that thought, I suddenly wanted him, despite the lingering pain. *Because* of the pain, in fact. I wanted him to stanch the stab of traitorous cells, to replace in me all that I had lost, to quicken love's fruit, send it sprouting from this branch of my vanquished family tree. Let this man usurp me, I thought, deny my rightful lineage.

"Jesus, Princess Sissy!" I imagined you cackling. "*Oh, fill me with your geeky seed!* Talk about privileging the hegemony of Euro-centric, male-dominated, fairy-tale heroics!" The pain, which had diminished to a dull ache, flashed. I fought it back.

To get me over my "squeamishness," as he termed it, Kyle insisted that I give him the insulin shot myself. He unbuckled his belt, tugged his pants down past his hips, and grinning lasciviously, instructed me to "give it to him."

"There," he coached, "right there. That's it. Nice and easy." I slowly thumbed the plunger. "Ah!" he sighed comically when I withdrew the needle. "Was it good for you, too?"

It was, I'm sure you'd snicker condescendingly to hear, an act that I found more intimate and touching than any of the mindless joinings of erogenous zones I'd heard you indulging in. So satisfying was that act, in fact, that I found my momentary desire for him strangely sated, sweetly dissipated, so that when Kyle, whose own dubious desire upon my arrival now seemed obversely enlivened by the shot, wrapped his arms around me and allowed that his bed was big enough for the both of us, I quieted any further urgings with a cool touch of my lips on his and bade him a demure goodnight at the bedroom door.

That night, while Kyle slept sleeping-bagged on the sofa in the next room, I curled in his bed, sheets still humid with the smell of him. I inhaled deeply. It was just a matter of time, I knew. Kyle would be mine. One day, he might replace the family that I'd lost. He would love and protect me, *need* me, cling to me and no other, and at long last (if I could marshal the strength to last that long!) I would be content. But with the click of the bedside lamp, the pain flickered within me, a darkly burning reminder that I had no future to dream of. My cancer taunted me, its promise unfolding like a flower. If it did not take me soon, it would surely take me after it had thrown its pollen to the wind, assuring its own immortality.

Later that night, I awoke, disoriented, and turned on the light. I opened the nightstand drawer, discovered a dog-eared copy of a particularly offensive men's magazine which, placed in my lap, fell open to a full-page "spread" of photos featuring a short-haired blonde performing cunnilingus on a rapturous brunette.

"When you kiss a frog," I heard you say, "you get warty lips." I felt dimly disappointed, yes, but in no way shocked. I understood Kyle's urges and felt partially responsible for his randy behavior. It was cruel and insensitive to hold out the promise of sex to him without deliverance, I told myself. A man had his limits. I should certainly know better by now.

I had, after all, grown up with an older brother.

·

Back at our apartment the next morning, I was met by your recentest conquest, that shirtless, shoeless, gym-shorted lout lounging on our sofa, bare heels propped on the coffee table. He grunted, scratched a hairy haunch, answered "Josh" to my obvious question, and returned his sleepy attention to the TV talk show he was watching.

"Sissy, *dar*ling," you gushed, emerging from the steamy bathroom, hair and body wrapped in towels. "Out all night, huh?" You giggled then, flung the towel from your head, proudly unveiling a damp ebony shag. "Tada!" you announced. "New 'do. Just finished it. I needed a change. How's it look?"

Stunned by the transformation, I was silent a moment too long. "It's you," I said, finally.

Your eyes fell, playfulness yielding to disappointment, disappointment to a dry smirk. "Thanks," you said flatly. "How very, like, *rumpled* we look this morning, Sissy-mine." You tousled your lover's hair, perched yourself on his lap, the towel parting, flashing a wedge of raven pubic hair before you closed it. Had you dyed that as well? I realized I hadn't the slightest clue to your true color. "There's a certain fire in the eyes, a glow to the face, a bow of the legs that, like, *screams* post-coital bliss! Say it isn't true," you sang. "Have we compromised our virtue?"

"That rhymes," Josh noted, shifting beneath you.

I bristled. "Don't start."

"Bet that's not what you told old Cal last night. Maybe *Slow down, not yet!*" You moaned, writhing in heartless sexual pantomime. "But pretty soon it was *Don't stop, oh, don't stop!*"

Josh smiled, guided your hips with his hands.

"You," I said wearily, turning toward my bedroom, "don't know the first thing about me."

But you followed, blocked the slammed door with a surprisingly sturdy shoulder, pushed your way in, suddenly angry.

"And how *should* I know anything about you," you ranted. "Have you once sat down to talk with me? No. I walk in and you give me this constipated grimace. You're like, 'Oh, I simply *must* study! I have so much *laundry* to do. Busy, busy, busy!' You know," you said, voice (impossibly!) catching, "I thought at first we could maybe be friends. I tried at first, but not *you*, not Miss Sissy Stoneface. I got a word of advice for you. Smile. Here's another. Play. Another. Eat. I got all *kinds* of words for you—*share!*—but you don't want to listen to a word I say." You shut teary eyes, hugged your towel around you. "How am I supposed to know the first thing about you when you won't even *talk* to me?"

My heart teetered. *There is a cancer in me,* I wanted to tell you. *I can feel it. It's been there as long as I can remember, tossing and turning in its sleep, and now it's finally awakened. You don't want to know me*, I almost said, but you'd probably just ask if I'd seen a doctor. *Jesus, Sissy*, you'd say, *it could be anything. Indigestion, appendicitis, diverticulitis, ovarian cysts. What is it with you and this cancer business?* And since you couldn't tell me anything I didn't already know, I chose to tell you nothing at all.

"You guys should kiss and make up," Josh said. He leaned in the doorway, upraised forearm resting on jamb, waistband sagging southward beneath hooked thumb. He cast an appraising eye at my bed. "I can help."

Your lower lip trembled. "This isn't working," you said, eyes still closed. "I should've advertised for a *human* roommate." You opened your eyes. "I want you out," you said, voice icy. "As soon as possible," you said. "Now."

I whirled, grabbed my book bag from the desk, bumped past the still-leering Josh.

"Maybe next time," he called after me.

•

Kyle was delighted with my decision to move in with him. "When?" he said.

"As soon as possible. I have classes all day, but I can move my things tomorrow."

"I'm free today. Give me your key, and I'll start in. I can't wait." Tentative fingers stroked my breast. I allowed him this promissory pleasure—a small gesture, really—before taking his wrist and turning his upturned palm to my lips. "This is going to be fun," he said, voice rasping.

He gave me a copy of his key; I gave him mine and a list of my monkish possessions.

"If she's there, tell her she can keep my deposit. Don't argue. Don't let her start anything."

"Don't worry," Kyle said, and, with a lingering, celebratory kiss, we parted.

After he left, the embryonic flutter of need he'd left me with slowly transmogrified into the pain I'd come to recognize. There is a kind of pain that signals unfinished business, a pain that is all the keener once one acknowledges that its throb represents irreparable damage rather than healing. There is the kind of pain that can be conquered only by relinquishing all hope of its cessation, for only death can take the pain away. It's a pain that puts life in perspective. It was this kind of pain—along with hunger pangs, since I'd eaten nothing all morning, and it was lunchtime now—that partially explains what I did next.

Solitary bachelor that he was, Kyle kept few edibles in his refrigerator: several cans of soda, a carton of non-dairy coffee creamer, the coffee itself, and various jars of condiments, lids long encrusted with their slopped contents. Eating would have to wait, I could see, though my appetite, perversely, seemed to peak at the sight of his filthy fridge. I took sponge and paper towel to shelves, racks, and bins, scrubbing months of neglect from their grimy surfaces.

And that's how I discovered the refrigerator's secret. There, at the back of the vegetable bin, slumping soggily behind a desiccated summer squash, lay a baggied, partial package of Oscar Mayer All-Beef Wieners. Five or six remained, as I recall, and, with some revulsion, I opened the bag, expecting they'd be past even Kyle's powers of consumption, but when I sniffed them, plucked one out to inspect for slime or mold, they seemed none the worse for wear. Perfect cinch-skinned sausages, I thought, ground to characterless conformity and shot through with preservatives; firm and fleshy, plump and boneless links of homogenous meat: the perfect food for the perfectly domesticated carnivore. I suppressed a giggle at the obvious phallic link, made to return wiener to baggie, when the pain cried out sharply.

Eat! my cancer demanded. *Jesus, Sissy, just a taste. Live a little. It's only a hot dog!*

Or so it seems in retrospect. Suddenly I was famished. I could not tell pain from hunger, knew only that both might cease with a single bite. I had not eaten meat since my father's death, and now, as I eyed this bland specimen pinched between thumb and forefinger, I salivated wildly, feral as its namesake. I put it to my lips, opened wide, bit down. The flavor was piercing, more exquisite than I remembered. I ate every dog in the package, gullet spasming, gagging on the final bite but swallowing anyway, gorging my pain and, ironically, abating it for the time being.

Then I went to class.

Midway through my professor's lecture on the rhetorical strategy of the assimilative oxymoron in early American captivity narratives, the pain returned, somewhat lower in origin.

"Are you all right?" she asked me when class was over, but I only nodded, gathered my books hastily, and ran to the restroom. I purged myself of the pink, stinking mess, splashed cold water on my face, but still felt no relief. I looked in the mirror: stricken eyes stared back into mine. My stomach twisted along with my snarling mouth. What had I done?

I knew then that it was not enough to rid myself of cancer's meat; I must replenish myself as well. I could not attend my second class feeling this way. I would go back to our apartment one last time, take from refrigerator and pantry shelves that which was rightfully mine, eat of the prescribed grains and fruits, fortify my will, and, if you were there, bid you firm adieu—in and out, no muss or fuss, never to return.

When I arrived, however, you were fellating Kyle, and that, of course, changed everything.

I stood silently in the doorway. Kyle sat on the sofa, muscles straining, unbuckled pants pulled below buckled knees. Perched prettily on the edge of an abandoned box of books, leaning into him, head bobbing, sat you. You were just finishing up, apparently, because Kyle suppressed a soprano squeal and collapsed backward, eyes tight, thin lips grimacing.

"Jesus *God*," he groaned, and then he saw me. His eyes stayed dazed for the slightest of breaths before panic rose to them, and he pushed your head roughly away. He stood, pulled up his jeans, zipped his fly. "It was her," he said, eyes imploring. "You have to believe me. I didn't want this. I didn't want any of it. Really, it wasn't me!"

"Must've been some other dick-head," you said, still seated. You wiped slick lips with the back of your hand, wiped hand on tail of untucked blouse. You looked at me then, smeared face empty of any recognizable emotion. "Care to join us?" you said, as if by rote. "After all, you primed the pump."

Though my first instinct was to run as fast and as far away as I could, my stomach betrayed me, suddenly wrenched, and pain slithered through my intestines. I was undone, and I barely made it to the bathroom before my pitiful bowels exploded in shame and misery.

You followed me in. "Hell of an entrance," you said, but you weren't smiling, and when Kyle appeared behind you, face twitching, unable to look me in the eye, unable to do anything but mumble my name, you elbowed him sharply back.

"Get out of here," you cried, slamming and locking the

door. "Jesus, Sissy," you sighed, and then you went to work.

You ran a bath, undressed me, helped me into the steaming water. You rinsed my soiled clothes in the sink, and then you took soap and washcloth to me, bathing me like a child. I remembered helping my father bathe my mother and, later, bathing my father's ruined body all by myself, my breath shallow against the stench of decay, but as you sudsed my limp, compliant limbs and trunk, nursely efficient, you never so much as wrinkled your nose. You drained the foul water, ran the tub full again, let me soak for a time while you used the sink to scrub your face and brush your teeth. You spit, stared at your unadorned reflection in the mirror, frowned.

"You never should've sent him for your stuff," you said. "Let me clue you: a guy moves your stuff, he thinks he owns you."

I found my voice, a small thing at the back of my throat. "I can't begin to imagine," I said, "how your mind works."

You shrugged. "He pissed me off."

"He pissed you off, so you sucked him off."

Your face clouded, and you turned away from yourself. "I'll tell you a secret," you said, eyes piercing. "I don't think I like men very much."

"Some secret," I murmured.

You washed and rinsed my hair then, raised me up and toweled me dry, lingering at my lower abdomen when I winced.

"Hurt?" you said, pressing lightly.

I made no answer.

"What's wrong with you?" you asked.

My eyes lowered. "I ate meat today."

You smiled slowly. "Bless you, Sissy, for you have sinned."

It wasn't until after you'd placed me in front of the mirror, wiped a circle free of fog, and stood behind me brushing my hair that you spoke again. "I didn't mean to hurt you, Sissy," you said. "Just the opposite, in fact. You know, you have really fine hair."

I stared at my own reflection, the afflicted eyes, the wounded mouth. "You can't hurt me anymore," I said.

You stopped brushing, turned me, naked and shivering, to face you. It was then I realized just how tiny you were—so perfect a miniature, your jet black bangs reaching no higher than my breastbone, so physically unintimidating, baby-doll cute. You were formed to spring, to twist and somersault, to balance the narrow path of elevated bar. There was nothing to fear in you.

"Look," you said, small hands gripping my shoulders, but I never let you finish. I doubled over, face burrowing into your neck, the pain a branding iron searing the cells deep inside me.

"Jesus, Sissy, you gotta go again?"

I gasped for air, wobbled my head no.

"We gotta get you to bed. You're one sick puppy."

Kyle, long gone now, frightened off by his own misspent passion, had already packed my bedding, so you took me to your room instead. I'd seen your eclectic decorating scheme from the doorway, but in the three months we'd shared apartment, I'd never set foot inside till now. Desert coral and turquoise vied with downeastern utility. A Navajo blanket, blood-red angles shot with black lightning, covered your brass bed. A cast iron wood-burner—unvented, unusable—pedestaled a jug-handled pot of dried cornstalk. Tiered lobster traps shelved books, curios, stereo. A makeshift easel of grey and weathered driftwood displayed a framed and glassed-in sand painting. Bright grains featured an Indian maiden riding a halterless Appaloosa, bitless teeth bared, her colorful skirts flying in the wind. "Painted Desert" the inscription read. Nothing more.

Had you lived in Arizona? Vacationed in Maine? I knew nothing of your origins.

You helped me between cool sheets, stopping just short, I imagined, of tucking me in and kissing my forehead. "Rest," you said, taking your leather notebook from the desk. "I have some work to do." And then you softly closed the door behind you.

I probed my lower abdomen, fingertips grazing pubic hair, searching for the source. This was the way it started, I knew, the curse of cellular mutation. It would take me one day soon, change me, replace me, leaving me nothing I'd recognize as ever having been truly mine. Slowly but inexorably, I would lose myself in its promise of everlasting transformation.

When I awoke, it was dark, and you were sitting on bed's edge, softly silhouetted by the light from the hallway. "Here," you said, holding a spoon to my mouth. Your cupped hand below it touched my chin. "Pepto. Not on your diet, but take your medicine like a good girl."

I swallowed pink chalk, sat up. You put the spoon on the bedside table. I saw that you'd changed into your nightgown, a girlish plaid flannel top with matching shorts. "Staying home tonight?" I said. "The boys won't know what to do with themselves."

You smiled. "Boys always know what to do with themselves." You shifted closer to me, one leg crooked beneath you. "Hey," you said. "I'm sorry, Sissy."

"My name isn't Sissy."

"Shit, I know that," you said, eyes dancing. "Think we can start all over?"

"Impossible."

Your face fell. "Here," you sighed, producing your leather notebook. "I wrote you something. Meantime, I got a pot of garlic soy soup stinking up the kitchen. Found it on your shelf. Package says it's good for you, but it smells like something died in there."

"Kyle says you're a dyke."

I'd meant to hurt you, but you only hesitated a moment, as if reconsidering, and then handed me the notebook. "It's the last one in there," you said, forcing a smile. "Read it and weep. I got some soup to stir."

And with that, you left. I switched on the bedside lamp, propped book on blanketed knees. I felt the medicine soothing my stomach, calming me, as I opened your pages. I started at the beginning, paged through your early entries, drafted and redrafted, crisp leaves of delicate longhand shot through with muscular X's, impatient arrows, rabid loops. Toward the end, I found the formative version of the poem inspired by my imagined genitalia, a lyrical delta of deletions and second thoughts entitled "Sissy's Seafood." Found also, following, those products of your recent writer's block, those poems you hadn't dared show me till now: "Sissy's Smallish Smile," "Sissy's Breasts, Her Hips," "Sissy's Greatest Hits, Her Misses," "Sissy's Whisper," "Sissy's Lips, Her Tongue," "Sissy's Hissy Fit," and, finally, the final first draft in the collection, the one you'd written today, unmediated by art's disapproving muse, unmarred by craft's niggling editor, unashamed of its unoriginality:

"Sissy's Sorrow"

I have sucked off
your boyfriend
who was in
my way
and who
you were helplessly
hoping
would save you

Nourish me
he was tasteless
so bland
and so tepid

I closed your notebook, hugged it low to my stomach, pressed it hard into me, as if to flatten and preserve the pain beneath it, make a loose-leaf memento mori of it.

What now? I thought. I was too weak to move, too smart to give Kyle another chance. Better to spike his insulin with Clorox than to spike you with his insulin. Besides, I'd doomed you already, smitten you as surely as if I'd poisoned those purloined nectarines, slit each open, tongued its glistening flesh, left cells of thriving cancer clinging to each pulped pit. And I'd doomed myself as well. We'd eaten of the same fruit.

We would be lovers, it was clear. If I were still in bed when you returned, if I could last that long, if you hadn't already reconsidered, revised this final poem, shed flannels for frills and waltzed out the door, eyes brightly carnivorous, pleasuring in the hunt and capture, all thoughts of me a dim distasteful reminder of a season's folly.

If I could last until the soup was done, we would be lovers. The fearful thrilling trill was there inside me, had lingered long after I'd lost my true loves. When you returned, if you returned, we would do the things that lovers do. You would teach me, and I would indulge your cruel craving, nurture it until it fit neatly inside the wanting place I'd been preparing for it.

"Let me tell you a secret," I imagined myself saying.

"Hush," you'd answer, bowl steaming in your hands. "Taste." You'd spoon warm broth to my mouth, press cool lips to my forehead, tongue darting, testing my fever. "Hot," you'd decide, and I'd lay helpless, hungry, burning up with budding blight. "Savor," you would say.

QUANTUM PHYSICS AND MY DOG BOB

The week before I started eighth grade, my father, tired of my "aimless ways" as he called them, decided to give me a project. "Today's Thursday," he said at breakfast. "You start school Monday," he went on as if I couldn't read a calendar. "I'll give you till Sunday to train that goddamn dog of yours to quit digging holes in my back yard." He opened his wallet, pulled out a hundred dollar bill. "Succeed and this is yours. Fail and you get dog shit."

"Dog shit?"

"Nada, zip, zilch, zero. You get a hole in the ground upside the house that fills with water after every rain and threatens the very foundation of this family's hearth and home. Understood?"

I rolled my eyes. "What family?" I muttered.

My mother had left us two months ago. It was just me and my father now.

"Don't get smart with me," he said. "I'm giving you four days. Come up with a plan of action, but don't think about it too long. Actions speak louder than blueprints." He tucked the hundred back in his wallet. "Go to it, son."

"It's not even my dog. It's Mom's dog."

"She left Bob with you."

"Who says?"

"I say. Look, son, I know you feel hurt and abandoned, but life goes on, and that dog is your responsibility now."

"I don't feel hurt and abandoned."

"Glad to hear it. Stiff upper lip and all that."

"She abandoned you, not me."

His lips curled in a thin smile. "That's the spirit."

"If we let him stay in the house, Bob wouldn't dig up the back yard," I said. "He's just bored, is why he does it."

My father shook his head. "Nice try but no go. People live in people houses. Dogs live in dog houses. It's been that way since the beginning of time, and I'm not about to buck the system by letting that animal eat and sleep in the alpha male's den. Especially not in the month of August in the great state of Florida when the fleas are at their fiercest. No, sir. Life is a series of boredoms, each mundane moment dragging its way inextricably towards the next, and your worthless dog's got to learn that digging holes in my back yard is no cure for the essential existential condition. And speaking of the essential existential condition, I have a committee meeting in an hour. Time for both of us to get to work."

I hated it when he talked like this. He was a philosophy professor at the university, and every conversation turned into a lecture. No wonder my mother had finally packed her bags and disappeared. She'd left a note, which I'd found crumpled up in the kitchen trashcan. "I can't live like this even one more day," it had said.

The note wasn't addressed to anybody in particular.

•

"I'm worried about him," I'd heard my mother say one night through the thin wall that separated our bedrooms. This was the year they'd skipped me a grade. "I wish he'd make some friends."

"Who needs friends?" my father grumbled. "I just wish he'd get his head out of his ass and do something useful."

"That," my mother said, "has got to be the most heartless thing I've ever heard."

"Stick around," he'd growled. "You ain't heard nothing yet."

The truth was, I was a dreamy kid, but I wasn't lazy, and I didn't need my father's project to keep me busy. I already had a project. I was secretly studying the latest developments in quantum physics. Had been all summer long. But I wasn't about to tell my father about my new interest, because next thing you know he'd be horning in and telling me what to read and what to do and lecturing me endlessly on the best way to prepare for my future, like he had the year before when I made the mistake of telling him math was my favorite subject in school and maybe I'd major in it when I went to college. Next thing I knew, he tried to put me to work discovering the highest known prime number.

"Didn't they already discover that?" I said.

"Well, of course, but there's always a higher one."

"Then what's the use?"

He frowned. "You'll never get anywhere with that kind of attitude," he'd told me.

Now, as far as my father was concerned, I wasn't interested in anything. But all the while he thought I was idly surfing the internet ("You'd better not be looking for porn!"), I was visiting university websites devoted to quantum mechanics, string theory, and supersymmetry. Revolutionary discoveries were being made at the subatomic level. Scientists were positing a universe that existed in eleven dimensions instead of the mundane four our senses restricted us to. Studies in particles and waves were paving the way for a Grand Unified Theory that would explain the workings of the whole universe. Humanity could soon cast off the shackles of time and space.

I wanted in on that.

But my computer was a sluggish old cast-off model my father had given me when he got an upgrade at the university. Sites took forever to load, and the thing crashed on me regularly. With a hundred bucks, I could buy more memory. So, reluctantly, I turned my attention to the problem of my dog Bob.

I spent the rest of the day in my room preparing myself, staring at my computer screen, trying to "think outside the box." I pulled up a few supersymmetry websites, browsed some physics newsgroups, tried to imagine what Bob might look like in eleven dimensions, but I was getting nowhere. I Googled "why dogs dig" and was not surprised to discover that the main reason was boredom, but all the cures involved an inordinate amount of effort on my part, from walking Bob two or three times a day to filling the existing holes with his own doggy poop and covering them back up. There had to be a better way.

I took a break from the Bob project and idly Googled my mother for about the hundredth time since she'd left—both her married and her maiden names, neither of which was especially common—but came up empty as usual. I'd Googled my father's name once and come up with pages and pages of results: articles written by him, articles written about him, awards won, prizes bestowed, degrees conferred…

But the fact was my mother had never done anything more notable than marry my father, give birth to me, and defend me daily from his incessant criticism. She was a stay-at-home mom until I started first grade, and after that she had a succession of jobs in retail, none of which she especially cared for and none of which she stuck with. My father periodically lectured her that she needed some kind of profession and that a profession demanded at least an undergraduate college degree, but my mother always responded that she'd finished her college career already.

She'd gone to exactly one year of college, where she was a student in my father's introductory Principles of Philosophy course. My father was fifteen years her senior, a confirmed bachelor prof, and so instantly struck by her beauty that he forgot all about the ethics of his profession and, before the semester ended, impregnated her with me, quite possibly in his university office—I shuddered to imagine. Subsequently recalling that he actually taught a graduate course in Ethics, he married her to make his transgression all better.

Of course it had taken me the better part of my insatiably curious sixth-grade year to piece together this story from each parent's official version and my own clandestine detective work, but suffice it to say that parents who think they're keeping origins secret from their kids are usually more in the dark than the kids themselves.

The hard truth was that my mother had been my only ally against my hypercritical father, and I had been her staunchest defender against her husband's condescending put-downs. And suddenly she was gone, and what was I supposed to do now?

I Googled "holes next to house foundation" and discovered a number of animals aside from Bob who might reasonably be held responsible for undermining our hearth and home, woodchucks and armadillos being the prime suspects. Had my father actually ever caught Bob in the act?

I was getting nowhere, and my head hurt. So I watched Youtube videos until my father came home for dinner.

He stood at the stove stirring a pot of Ragu spaghetti sauce straight from the bottle. "Any progress?" he said.

"I'm still thinking."

He curled his lip. "Thinking," he echoed. "You've been thinking all day, son. The time for thinking is past. Do you think Ho Chi Minh was thinking when he launched the Tet Offensive?"

"I'm twelve years old, Dad."

"Do you think Mozart was thinking when he was twelve years old? No. He was too busy composing concertos for flutes and strings and things. He was a boy of action."

"You wanna cut me some slack, please?"

"Sure thing," he said. "I live to cut you slack. But let me tell you something, young man. Once you get out in the real world, nobody's going to be cutting you any slack. The world cuts slack for no man."

"Yeah, yeah, yeah."

"Don't you yeah me. Nobody yeahs me, least of all my own son. Am I understood?"

"Okay already."

"And get with the program," he said, dumping a box of Muellers into the pot of boiling water. "Set the table. Pour our water. Do I have to tell you every goddamn day?"

•

After my father left for work Friday, I decided it was time to study the problem a bit more closely, so I found a dog biscuit and ventured into the back yard. I hated our back yard. Great double-pronged weeds sprouted from the un-mowed lawn. Algae bloomed in the cracks and flaking marcite patches of our kidney-shaped pool. In the mulched bed bordering the pool, the begonias my mother had planted last hopeful spring were shriveled tufts of straw surrounded by hardened piles of Bob poop. It was only mid-morning, but the air was already a blast furnace, the sun a sledgehammer pounding on the anvil of my brain. No wonder Bob had resorted to digging holes in the yard. Not only did it give him something to break the tedium, but the earth was cooler a couple of feet below the surface.

I called for him. No answer. I checked his dog house, cramped and stuffy, and wasn't surprised to find it empty. I checked his favorite hole, dug next to the southwest corner post of our stockade fence. No Bob. I checked three of his other holes. Still no Bob. Finally, I discovered him in a freshly-dug hole beneath the overgrown hedges at the very back of the yard. He sprawled there, panting, and raised his head to eye me noncommittally.

"Here, boy," I said, and held out the biscuit.

Bob slowly grunted his way to his feet and exited the bushes. When I gave him the biscuit, he settled himself stiffly in the calf-high stalks of dry and brittle crabgrass, gnawing listlessly. He was a mixed breed my mother had rescued from the pound when he was just a puppy to give to me for my fourth birthday. Once he grew to become a long-haired, mud-colored, eighty-pound mutt who chewed up every garden hose and pool float we owned, who would stand when I said "Sit!" and lie down when I said "Fetch," I lost interest in him. Bob was fat and lethargic. He barely wagged his sluggish tail when I scraped table scraps into his food bowl.

Bob finished the biscuit and began to lick at a sore on his hind leg. He'd had the sore for half a year now. Before she left, my mother had occasionally gazed out the back window, sighed wearily, and mentioned that she needed to take Bob to the vet one of these days when she found the time. I should have known something was wrong then.

I mopped sweat from my face with the front of my t-shirt. It was blistering hot. Ironically, I realized, the solution to all Bob's problems—heat, boredom, sores, even the torment of fleas—lay in plain sight before him every day of his pathetic doggy life, if only Bob would learn how to swim. But Bob was deathly afraid of going in the pool. Back when he was just a pup, he'd accidentally fallen in, panicked, and nearly drowned before my mother fished him out with the skimmer. No one had been able to coax him back into the water to date. My father tried throwing him in once and received a nasty bite in return.

"Your fucking dog," he'd told my mother as she cleaned and bandaged the wound, "is the most incorrigibly useless excuse for a pet I've seen in the history of the planet."

"It's not his fault," she said.

"Then whose fault is it? We live in a world of accountability. Things are always somebody's fault. Keep that mutt away from me," he'd growled. "I hate the sight of him."

I didn't have any more use for Bob than my father did, but I didn't hate him. I pitied him. What a life, cooped up day after pointless day with nothing to do but bake in the heat, scratch fleas, and lick sores. If I had to live like that, I'd seriously consider suicide. And who knew? Maybe Bob *had* considered suicide. Maybe he considered it daily. Maybe the high point of his life would be figuring out a way to do himself in without benefit of opposable thumbs.

Suddenly, a plan crystallized. I ran to the gate, unlatched it, swung it wide open. "Come on, boy!" I called. "Here, Bob!"

I coaxed, my voice laced with promise. "You're free, boy. Free! Run away! Run far, far away! You're free, Bob! Run!"

Bob stared at me, got to his feet, strolled back to his hole beneath the hedges and settled himself in for the rest of the afternoon.

·

"Looks like my hundred's safe," my father told me Saturday morning.

I moped in my room most of the day, not even bothering to boot up my computer. What was the use? There was no changing Bob. There was no finding my mother. There was no escaping my father. There was nothing I could do about anything.

As evening came on, my father banged on my bedroom door. "We're cooking out tonight, son," he said. He was drinking a can of beer and looked unaccountably cheerful. "Help the old man fire up the grill."

"Do it yourself."

My father glowered at me. "You'd better watch your step, young man."

"Watch your own step."

"What in the world is wrong with you?"

"You!" I shouted. "I had a perfectly good mother, and you broke her. You drove her off. You made her hate you, and then you made her hate me too!"

I was sobbing now. My father stood silent, eyes lowered, fists clenching and unclenching. "She didn't hate you," he said.

"She left me. She didn't even say goodbye."

My father considered this for a while, eyes far away. Then he blinked. He blinked again, as if suddenly awakened. "One moment," he said. He went next door to his bedroom, where I heard a drawer open and close. When he came back, he was holding a folded up sheet of paper. "This was taped to your door. Apparently she couldn't face you either."

He handed it to me. My name was on the outside, flanked by hearts. It was my mother's writing. I unfolded it and read:

My sweet dear heart,

> *I love you so much it hurts and it hurts even worse to do what I have to do now but I just have to leave or go crazy. I wish I could take you with me but I don't even know where I'm going and that's no kind of life for you now but my darling I promise I PROMISE once I get my feet on the ground I'll come back for you.*
>
> *All my love forever and ever,*
>
> *Mom*

My tears blurred the lines as I read it again and again.

"So obviously," my father said, "your mother never hated you."

"Why didn't you show me this?"

"I planned to," he said, "eventually. Once you were old enough to understand."

"Understand what?"

He shook his head, grimacing. "Your mother will never get her feet on the ground."

"Says you."

He drew himself up, put on his professorial face. "Yes. Says me."

"You don't know that. You don't know everything."

"Is this the way it's going to be from now on?"

I looked at the floor. *Till I'm old enough to leave myself,* I thought, but all I did was shrug. It was all I could manage.

"No, son, I don't know everything," he said. He sighed, put a hand on my shoulder. It felt heavy, and I stiffened under its weight. He withdrew his hand, stood arms akimbo. "But close enough. I know your mother. I know she's gone for good. And I know it's time we got over her." He turned and strode to the door. "Now come on, toughen up. Let's try to lighten the mood around here, okay? Let's do that barbecue."

•

I got the bag of charcoal from the garage, met him on the poolside patio, and watched him douse the coals with half a can of lighter fluid. I stepped back when he lit a match. The grill ignited with a blistering poof.

"Fetch me my tongs," he said.

"What's the magic word?"

He eyed me with dark surprise. "Please," he said. "Please make yourself useful."

I fetched his tongs and his long-handled fork, his apron and oven mitt, another cold beer, and when he deemed the time right, I brought him the T-bones he'd been marinating since mid-afternoon when the happy notion of having a little picnic with his only son apparently first dawned on him. He tonged a steak from the plate.

"The fire's still too hot," I said. "You'll burn them. We should wait a bit."

"Wait, wait, wait," my father said. "Think, think, think. A man wants meat, a man cooks meat. Period." He slapped the steaks on the grill, and tongues of flame leaped and sizzled. Suddenly Bob roused himself from the hedges. He strolled over, tail wagging, tongue lolling, and stood at my side expectantly.

"Keep that mutt back," my father complained when Bob jostled his leg. He raised his beer can, guzzled it dry, tossed the empty into the high weeds. "Get me another, son," he said.

"What am I, your own personal bartender?"

He shrugged. "I'll get it myself. Gotta visit the little boy's room anyway." He took off his mitt, tossed it at me. It hit me in the chest and fell to the deck. "Keep an eye on the steaks," he said. "Make sure not to burn 'em."

"What a jerk," I said to Bob after my father had gone inside. "Isn't he a jerk, Bob?" I said. "Isn't he? Huh? Yes, he is, Bob. Yes, Bob, yes he is. He'll always be a jerk."

Bob wagged his tail wildly, nearly dancing with excitement. He looked at the steaks blazing on the grill, looked at me, looked at the steaks again. He barked a gruff plea.

That's when the brainstorm hit me.

"Want a steak, Bob?" I said. "Huh? Do you, boy? Huh?"

Bob tilted his head at me, wagged his tail faster.

I got the tongs, picked a T-bone off the grill, held it high in the air. The juice dripped on the deck at Bob's feet. He licked the drips, then leaped at me, nearly knocking me over. I held the steak just out of reach. Bob barked, sprang again, but I was too quick for him. Then I jumped, fully clothed, into the shallow end of the pool. I waded out several feet and turned around, steak held forward. Bob stood at the pool's edge, slavering.

"Here it is, boy," I said. "Come and get it." I waved the steak around in what I considered to be a tantalizing circle. "Here's your steak, Bob. Come in the pool, boy!"

Bob just stared at me, and I could see the realization hit him. His tail curved straight up at attention as he stood there paralyzed with indecision, his poor little canine brain feeding a looped message around and around the inside of his pointy skull: STEAK GOOD, WATER BAD, over and over, thesis and antithesis with no synthesis in sight, "Here, Bob, c'mon,

Bob," body frozen in place like a bronzed tribute to Approach/Avoidance Syndrome, "Here's your steak, Bob," no barking, no drooling even, just staring, fixed in the inertia of uncertainty, "Come and get it, Bob," WATER BAD, STEAK GOOD, until I swear I could feel the kinetic energy vibrating like a plucked string at the subatomic level, particles spinning, waves radiating, dimensions folding in on themselves in search of the Grand Unification Theory that might allow Bob to have his steak without getting wet.

I heard a buzzing in my ears.

I wouldn't have been surprised to see Bob walk on water at this point, but instead what I saw seemed even more impossible.

Suddenly and spontaneously, Bob burst into flames.

He ran howling in circles around and around the pool deck, knocking over the grill and starting a minor brush fire in the tall dry weeds that my father later (and with some difficulty) put out with our leaky garden hose. By the time I got out of the pool, tackled Bob, and dragged him back into the pool with me, it was too late. The vet said that the burns themselves would have been treatable but that poor Bob had succumbed to shock.

When I told my father how it happened, that Bob had spontaneously combusted, he just shook his head. He'd seen the whole thing from the kitchen window, he claimed. "Bob went for a steak, knocked over the grill, and caught on fire. That's all."

"No," I said. "That's not the way it happened. He started on fire before he ever went near the grill. The fire started inside him. It was a chain reaction. He was stuck between what he wanted to do and what he couldn't do. He felt unbelievably torn."

"Rubbish," my father said. "Dogs don't feel anything.

Not like people do." He gripped my shoulder with one hand, squeezing hard. In the other hand he held a crisp new hundred dollar bill. He waved it slowly before my eyes before tucking it into my shirt pocket. "Not like you and me."

WAY

My mother taught my father the ways of the Dineh, Blessing-way to Enemy-way. Tse, she told him: Rock. Asdzaa: Woman. Bilagaana: White Man. Changing Woman, Spider Woman, Spider Rock, Rock Canyon: Tsegi. She sang the song of Talking God, but my father never listened. The day she left him, note knifed high on hogan door, his beat pick-up rutted the dirt lot outside Mrs. Yazzie's fourth-grade trailer, horn howling. He whooped for me to get my ass in gear: Pronto, Tonto!

"You're drunk," I said.

"Not near enough."

We raced across the Painted Desert, cactus and creosote leeching rock's blood, to Gallup, New Mexico, Land of Enchantment and drunk-ass Dineh, Lords of the Earth down on their luck. He sidled up to the dark-scarred bar where he'd met my mother twelve years ago, stomped sheep dung off his boots, ordered a shot and a beer, eyes burning. He couldn't believe, he told me, that for one chaps-slapping, spur-jangling night sharing his bedroll with that whisper-thin gal who'd lured him, drunken, to the heart of the Navajo Nation—sweet shadow, my mother, breathing bright spirits at the base of Spider Rock, twin spires stabbing the stars—for that single night, this cowboy got saddled the rest of his live-long days and fall-down nights with me. She put her brand on him, he said. Wove a web of wordless woman magic he galloped smack dab into. Lassoed him, reined him in, tethered him to rock, canyon, hogan, and now she'd up and left.

He knocked back another shot, took off his Stetson, burr-cut noggin near shrunken without it. Hell, he said, he'd do it all over: the drinking, the stars, Spider Rock, sheer canyon walls echoing my mother's gasps. He'd gladly shoulder the yoke of me for one more night like that with my mother. "But she's gone," he said, "gone for good. And what're we supposed to do now?"

Enemy-way and Yeibichei, she'd taught him, and it all came down to this.

I pulled a handful of corn pollen from my pocket and blew it in his wasted face. "What do you mean 'we,' white man?"

SPIDER ROCK

Driving down from the foothills of the Lukachukai Mountains, down, down towards Chinle. Still a good hour away. Catch glimpses of the del Muerto arm of the canyon soon enough, and then the dry red basin that holds the dusty crossroads town, one of the largest communities in the Navajo Nation.

For a while, though, all will be evergreen and blue, blue sky and snow beginning to melt down the bright slope.

Casey at the wheel of the school's station wagon. Car full of Navajos. Three little Navajo boys sitting next to him in the front seat. Three little Navajo girls sitting with Elise in back. Way back in the rear view mirror, stump forward, needles snagging the roof upholstery, point hanging some four feet out the open tailgate, lies the freshly cut Navajo Christmas tree. Pine scent fills the car. Happy holidays on the reservation. Elise says the kids have to have a real Christmas *sometime*. May as well be now. She's even teaching her class Christmas songs. Who knows? It might snow in Chinle come the twenty-fifth. Yuletide carols being sung by a choir and folks dressed up like Eskimos.

Everybody knows.

Two little Navajo boys sitting closest to the door—Michael and Auston—giggling low in their throats. Making jokes to each other in another language. Shooting low-lidded glances at Casey. He catches a word. *Bilagáana.* Means *white man.* Making jokes about his beard, probably. His blond hair. His whiteness.

Kid next to him—Goldwater—holding himself aloof. Good. Casey likes that. Goldwater can afford to ignore the kids next to him. They're afraid of him.

Much giggling from the back, too. Elise asking the girls questions. Girls answering in whispers, ducking their heads, laughing. Deborah, Belladonna, and one other whose name he can't remember. Doesn't matter.

Navajos never give the white man their real names anyway.

Strange carload. Kids are at that age where boys who hang out with girls are called sissies. Boys won't sit with girls. Won't look at them. Won't talk to them. Casey's gone through that stage himself. Seems universal.

The road winds down in front of Casey.

Goldwater stretching, all nonchalant, reaching slowly, trying to sneak a smoke from Casey's pack on the dashboard. Tough to be subtle about it.

Casey nudges him, lowers his brows. "Spider Woman come get you tonight," he says.

Goldwater sits back, says not a word.

Casey squeezes his knee. "Hey, I'm only kidding."

"Just one?" whispers Goldwater.

"I'll get in trouble."

Goldwater glances over his shoulder, purses his lips.

Casey will never get over it: Navajos really *do* point with their lips instead of their fingers, a whole different language.

"What can *she* do?" says Goldwater. His voice is so low.

"She'll kick my ass," says Casey.

A hoarse noise comes from Goldwater's throat.

Elise leans forward. "Is he trying to get a cig from you?"

"No," says Casey. And he smiles.

•

White man's not right on the reservation. Painted Desert flashes bloody teeth, frowns a red, dry, crusty frown at him all day long. Something tells him. This ain't Arizona, it says. This here's the moon. This here's a different world entire. You don't know, white man. This here's the *Dinétah*, the land of the people. This here's the Navajo Nation.

Yes, indeed. The *bilagáana* best beware. This land ain't loved no white man since Kit Carson burned the canyon. Canyon walls still weep. Tears run right to the floor. History dries up quick, white man, but you can read the message in the rusty streaks. It sure as hell ain't in the movies.

Casey can understand. He may be white—whiter than ever since he's been living here—but he's no fool. White man's got to lay low. Actions speak louder than words, is what the desert tells him. White man without a job has to keep that low profile, hope that nobody notices, hope that something comes up. No white man's getting a job when there's a shit house full of unemployed natives. White man keeps silent, gets into no trouble. Can't act like a tourist come to see the famous Canyon de Chelly, buy a few sand paintings, eat a Navajo pizza, soak up the local color. Must act like he lives here. Keep silent. Play like he's got depths, too. Just like the Navajo.

White man drinks.

•

Elise's back from her drive to Gallup. Nearest town off the reservation. Sixty miles away. Enters the trailer like a black-haired eastern breeze, head high, nighttime in her wake, all cool and soft and civilized. You can take the New Yorker out of New York, but… Got two cases of beer in the car, she says. Got a bottle of Jack Daniel's in hand.

So nice to see her, is what Casey says. "I was worried. It took you a long time."

Not to worry though because the dark's locked tight outside and all's cozy inside and though the wind slashes at the windowpanes, the only thing that gets in is a little red dust. Nothing stops that.

They drink. They smoke a joint. They drink.

The trailer creaks. Casey says it's a dumb-ass law, anyway, no liquor on the reservation.

"They can smoke peyote," says Elise.

Casey says he doesn't care, liquor prohibition is just plain old discrimination.

Elise shakes her head. "It's a Navajo law."

Casey's surprised. Thought the Bureau of Indian Affairs made the law. You know, oppressing the redskin and all.

Elise says no. "The Indian metabolism is different from ours," she says. "Low blood sugar, I think. They get drunk real easy."

"Come *on*! That's gotta be a myth."

"It's a medical fact. Just like the Japanese and Chinese can't drink much."

"Where'd you read this?"

"Somebody told me. I forget who. Anyway, it's true. It's genetic. Just like they have fat cheeks and can't grow hair on their faces."

Well, you can't argue genes. And Elise's lived here longer than he has. Who knows?

"Everybody knows," says Elise. "It's a fact."

•

Station wagon squealing around a sharp bend.

"You better slow down," says Elise.

Trees flashing by. Road curving and curving. Takes most of Casey's attention. One hand steering. Other hand lighting his cigarette. Out of the corner of his eye, Casey sees Goldwater staring at him out of the corner of *his* eye. The edges of their lines of vision brush lightly against each other.

"Do you really think so?" Elise is saying.

He looks up. Elise's beautiful face smiling at him in the rearview mirror. Black-topped heads bouncing in and out of view to either side of her. Elise bends low out of the mirror's range. Whisperings. Soft, childish laughter.

"Why don't you tell him so?" Elise murmurs.

Casey glances back. "What's happening, folks? Enjoying the ride?"

Big black eyes go wide on small, round, brown faces. Lips tighten, explode in giggles. They burrow into Elise's sides.

Adorable.

"They think you're handsome," says Elise.

Goldwater makes a hoarse noise low in his throat. It's kind of like a growl only sharper but all full of breath, too, and ending with an abrupt, back-of-the-palate, soft *k* sound. As far as Casey knows, this may be a real Navajo word. In context, it could mean anything from *fuck you* to *what an asshole you are* to *life's a bitch, ain't it?* to *I don't give a shit.*

"Don't talk to them," whispers Goldwater.

Casey bends slightly, keeping watch on the road. These kids all have such low voices. "Why not?"

"They're stupid. They're girls."

Casey straightens, smiles. "A couple of years from now you won't think they're so stupid. You'll be falling all over yourself trying to talk to them."

Goldwater makes that noise again. Another definition for the strange guttural. Don't tell me about the future, white man.

•

Sun's high in the Arizona sky. Casey's sweating, leaning on the metal railing like every other tourist, surveying with fresh eyes the vast, ravaged wound in the heart of the earth that is the Canyon de Chelley. Sightseeing.

Maybe a dozen people in all on the ledge of Spider Rock Overlook. Ten of these white. Much camera work going on. Some turquoise trinkets being bought from the old Navajo lady and little girl whose territory this must be. Tourists out for a bargain. Interstate 40's lined with raggedy looking shops and stands that sell real, honest-to-goodness Navajo jewelry, but you have to hit the backstreets of the reservation for the cut-rate prices.

Friend of Elise's makes a nice piece of money selling Navajo turquoise and silverwork. Buys up bracelets and necklaces and belt buckles off-season cheap. Makes a trip to Los Angeles once a month. Market's good there, he says. Demand's so high and supply's so low, you can deal two hundred percent markup easy.

Casey met the man last night. Teaches just across the hall from Elise at the Elementary. Big red-haired dude. Hails from Iowa City. Name of Roger Hook. Likes to have the kids call him Captain.

Har.

Just dropped in to bum a few of the beers that, rumor had it, Casey picked up on his drive through Illinois. Pumped

Casey's hand too hard. Talked too loud. Guffawed like a mule.

"So you're the New York stud little Elise's been saving herself for."

Casey smiled, said something about how as far as he knew Elise had sufficient self to spare that she needn't save any of herself for anybody. But he was glad to hear that she'd at least saved herself from *this* one.

"Hee-yuck!" Hook told him.

Casey wished that Hook had a volume knob in the middle of his throat so he could turn him down. Hook guzzled Casey's beers. Told some corny "Navajo" jokes. How come Jesus wasn't born on the reservation? They couldn't find three wise men and a virgin. Seemed like he'd never leave. Casey played three games of backgammon with him. Lost twenty-eight bucks. Finally, apparently satisfied, Hook left. Chuckling all over himself.

Casey told Elise that Roger Hook was a pain in the ass.

"What about you?" she countered. "You were rude as hell. What kind of first impression do you think *you* made?"

"I don't care what kind of first impression I made. He's a jerk."

"Come on," she said. "He's my friend. He's not so bad. You're just pissed because he beat you."

"I don't mind losing," said Casey. "I just don't like how much he enjoys winning. Christ, he foams at the mouth. Anybody who enjoys winning that much enjoys other people losing even more. And what the hell is this *Captain* bullshit? How you can hang around with such a moron?"

Elise told him there weren't that many people for her to hang around with in Chinle, and besides, she'd appreciate it if he wouldn't call her friends morons. She could damn well hang around with anybody she wanted to.

Oh, and it looked to be an unfriendly night last night, right up to bedtime, with Casey staring silently at Elise's long, lovely, tense back until he could take the silence no longer and touched the knot between her shoulders and said how he was sorry, he didn't mean anything by anything he said, and felt the knot unravel as she turned to him. Then the night was fine. Just fine.

•

Grey-haired tourist nudging Casey. Camera dangles mid-paunch. Strap folds sunburned skin across back of neck. Tourist spreads arms wide at the canyon before them.

"Magnificent, huh?"

"Yeah," says Casey.

"You know, we took in the Grand Canyon on our way here. This is nothing compared to the Grand Canyon."

Casey nods, turns his back, walks to the other end of the railing. Somebody always wants to spoil your trip. Nothing? How can you compare anything to the incomparable?

Day before yesterday, his second day on the reservation, Casey visited White House Ruins, far down the canyon, just outside of Chinle. Got the guided tour, too, by this young Navajo who said he was a part-time student at Tsaile Community College. Studying agricultural engineering. They grow all kinds of crops on the canyon floor, he said. White House Ruins set securely in a huge pockmark halfway up the canyon wall. Gleaming blindingly in the sun. Remnant of some older civilization. Pueblo dwellers. Long gone now. Guide said they were the *Anasazi*. Meant *old dudes that left* in Navajo talk. Or something like that. Casey wanted to know where they got all that white mud to make their houses, this canyon being so red and everything. Guide just laughed. They climbed authentic rickety ladders to get to the place and the ruins were so authentically old and ruined and Casey was amazed. Simply amazed.

Far, far below is the canyon floor and right in the middle of it sprouting tall and wide and not giving a shit about anything in this world but itself is Spider Rock. Two bloody fingers of sandstone, joined at their base, point high, poke the sky in the eye. Makes a person stand and stare all open-mouthed and glassy-eyed because it just defies you to gain some kind of perspective on it, fit it into your frame of reference. Casey's seen tourists do the same thing checking out the World Trade Center from the bottom up. And this is supposed to be nothing? Spider Rock has to be bigger than anything man-made.

He consults his guidebook. Not a book, really. A copy of *Arizona Highways* that Elise gave him. Special feature on the Canyon de Chelley. Good magazine. Lets him know that it's pronounced *shay*, not *shelley*. Which is nice.

Book says the tallest spire of Spider Rock is eight-hundred feet from floor to pinnacle. Eight-hundred feet and they call it a rock. Still, it's not as tall as he thought. Goddamn Grand Canyon.

New group of tourists coming up behind him, pointing and gasping. Spider Rock doesn't care. Point all you want. Gasp your last gasp. I ain't going nowhere.

Here's something. Book says Spider Rock's really called *Tse Na'ashje'ii*. Casey won't even try to pronounce that one. It's named after this goddess *Na'ashje'ii Asdzaa*. Navajo tongue sure does put a strangle-hold on English phonetics. It means Spider Woman.

Casey likes that. He reads.

Seems Spider Woman used to be the goddess of weavers. More than that, he sees, she was instrumental in helping the twin gods Monster Slayer and Child Born of Water perform some difficult—and unspecified—tasks so they could get to see the Sun, their father, and find out what they had to do to kill off the monsters that were eating up all of the earth people way back when.

Thus, he reads, was this, the fourth world, set up.

A rather spotty account. What were the first three worlds? What were the tasks? How did Spider Woman help? What did the Sun know that everybody else didn't and why was he holding back the information?

Spider Rock ain't telling.

A tug at his sleeve. Casey turns to see the little Navajo girl. She shows him an arm strung with beads.

"Two dollars," she says.

Casey buys a strand. Then, on a whim, "Tell me about the Spider Woman," he says.

The girl's eyes widen. She retreats.

Nearby, the old Navajo woman laughs. "You frighten the child," she says.

"I didn't mean to. What did I say?"

"Spider Woman live on Spider Rock, on top." The woman points. Casey nods. "She weave web, swing down at night. She come into hogan, take away bad children. She take them to top of Spider Rock, eat them up." The woman laughs and laughs.

Some of the tourists are gathering around. Taking pictures. A slice of the wild west to bring home from vacation. Write it on the back of the print. Old Navajo woman telling American Indian legends—Canyon de Chelley National Monument, Arizona.

Casey wonders if the woman's putting on the broken

English. Injun talk for the white folks. Maybe she's seen too many Lone Rangers.

"I thought she was a goddess," says Casey.

The woman makes a strange breathy sound in the back of her throat. "Old fashioned religion," she says. "Spider Woman just scare children now." She laughs and laughs and laughs.

Casey, holding his magazine rolled up tight, turns away. Spider Rock looms before him. No goddess stands atop it. Position's open. Send résumé to Foundation for Cultural Renewal, Navajo Nation.

·

Elise teaches all day. Bringing home that bacon. Winning that bread. Meanwhile, Casey plays house. He gets up when she leaves and he does some pushups and sit-ups. He makes the bed. He washes last night's dishes. He gets out the vacuum cleaner and tries to suck up as much of the fine red silt that's collected overnight in the carpet as he can. He wipes red dust off the tables and chairs and windowsills. It always comes back.

He goes to the bathroom, sits on the can for twenty minutes with a cup of coffee and a cigarette and a book. He stands at the mirror and debates whether he should shave his beard. Getting kind of scraggly looking. People will stare. He decides not to and takes a shower.

Every day.

And each day is beginning to blend inseparably into the next. Like a low rolling fog.

What did you do today, Casey?

Oh, nothing.

Yeah? Did you have a good time?

Oh, not bad. Casey remembers reading somewhere that the Hopi Indians, a neighboring tribe of the Navajo, speak a language that has no past or future tenses. Only the present. Always now. It sounded fairly impossible at first, but Casey's getting the hang of it now. Yes, he is.

Every day.

He goes to the supermarket to buy supper for tonight. It's about a mile walk. He passes cattle crossing the street. Flocks of sheep. Old Navajo women dressed in motley silks. No one speaks to him. He speaks to no one.

The supermarket's always crowded. Few white faces. An undercurrent buzz and bumble of Navajo talk. He stands before the butcher's counter, waiting. An old woman, her face beaten, scrunched, and jowls hanging all over wrinkles and sun cracks, gives the butcher her order.

They speak in Navajo. Casey has no idea. They could be talking about anything. He stands tall and glaze-eyed, indifferent.

The woman leaves. Casey steps forward.

"I'd like a pound of hamburger, please."

The butcher stares at him. Dark, dark, high-cheeked face. Black oily hair. Blood stains on a white apron.

"Number," says the butcher.

Casey doesn't understand.

The butcher taps the top of the machine on the counter beside Casey.

Automation on the reservation.

Casey pulls a ticket from the machine. It's got perforated edges. It says: 37.

The butcher flips a cardboard placard on a ring hanging behind him.

"Thirty-seven," he says.

Casey hands him the ticket. He tries to make his voice go lower, more gravelly in tone. "Pound of hamburger," he says.

•

Casey sits in the living room, reading. Suddenly Elise's slamming through the door all excited. Raindrops drip from her head to the floor. Red mud tracks the clean carpet. The Yeibichei Dancers came to her class today, she's saying.

"God, Casey, I think I was as scared as the kids were!"

"What happened?" says Casey.

"They beat up one of my kids!"

"Why? What happened?"

Elise explains. The Yeibichei Dancers used to be big medicine a long time ago. Still are, really. They dress up like ghosts and dance special ghost dances and call on spirits and cure the sick and everything. They got the powerful hoodoo and canyon spooks working for them. But another thing they do is play like bogeymen to keep the kids in line. Periodically the Yeibichei dress up and go to school and come running, dancing, leaping all wild and ferocious into a classroom and the kids all hide under their desks and the teacher says nothing and does nothing and the Yeibichei grab a kid or two—it's said that the parents supply the names of the bad ones—and beat the kid with whips and sticks.

"They really did it, too!" says Elise, all out of breath. "They dragged this poor kid Goldwater out in front of the class and they really *whipped* him."

"What did you do?" says Casey.

"I didn't know *what* to do. We're not supposed to interfere."

"What did this kid do?"

"What the fuck do you *think* he did? He was screaming and crying and begging me to help him. God, it broke my heart."

Casey sees she's upset, so he puts his arms around her and tells her it's all right. "It's just a different culture. Different practices."

Elise says she knows.

"Why did they pick on this kid—what's his name?"

"Goldwater."

Casey laughs. "What kind of name is that?"

"It's his Anglo name."

"His parents must be good Republicans."

"His father's a fucking drunk. Sometimes Goldwater comes into school drunk, too. I'm sure. He's the worst kid in the class. He's always picking fights and he's big for his age so most of the kids are scared of him. He sniffs glue, too."

Casey tisks, shakes his head. "How do you know?"

"Some of the kids told me. They said he was trying to make them do it."

"Did they?"

"Probably. They're not exactly angels either. Anyway, the Yeibichei hear about all this shit, somehow."

Casey strokes her hair, massages the muscles in her neck. "Listen," he says, "don't worry about it. It's not your job. Maybe it was a good lesson for the kid. Hey, come on, you're too tense. Do you want to smoke a joint?"

•

Coming into the canyon area now. No more trees. No more snow. Air still has a nip to it, but Casey's got the window rolled down a crack to let the cigarette smoke out of the car. Road shines slick and full of puddles. Must have rained while they were in the mountains. Chinle will be a mud hole when they get there.

Wet red earth to the left dotted with dull green bushes and brush-weed, rising for a hundred yards or so and dropping off out of sight into the canyon. Short horizon. River will be running stronger down there now. Soon enough the farmers and herders will have to make their annual move from the floor to the rim. That or get swept away.

Elise and the girls singing in back. Elise's sweet alto carrying the tune and most of the lyrics. God rest ye, merry gentlemen. Let nothing you dismay.

Casey nudges Goldwater, points to his left. "You got any people down there?"

Goldwater nods.

"Close relatives?"

Remember Christ our Savior was born on Christmas day.

"An uncle," says Goldwater.

"You visit him much?"

Goldwater shrugs. "River's rising."

To save us all from Satan's thrall when we were gone astray.

Casey flicks an ash out the window. "Must be beautiful living down there."

"Can't live there in the winter," Goldwater says.

"Yeah, but in the summer."

O-oh tidings of comfort and joy, comfort and joy.

"Too much quicksand in the summer," says Goldwater. "He loses a lot of sheep."

Elise stops singing. "Hey! You guys sing with us."

Auston rolls his eyes, mumbles something to Michael. Goldwater takes a deep breath.

"Come on! You learned the words in class."

"Forgot," says Goldwater.

"No you didn't. Casey, you sing, too. We need some bass."

Casey laughs. "I think I'm a tenor," he says. "Besides, I don't think I ever learned this one."

"Let's sing 'Jingle Bells' then. Everybody knows that one, right?

Belladonna, Deborah, and that other little girl all say that they do.

"Don't sing," Goldwater whispers to Casey. "It's stupid."

Elise leans forward. Casey feels her hair fall on his shoulder. "Oh!" she says. "I didn't realize that you were too *smart* to sing. I wouldn't want you to do anything *stupid*." She sits back. "The boys think singing's stupid. Do you think we can manage without their deep, masculine voices?"

The girls all agree that they can. It's fine with them. They don't need the stupid boys anyway.

"Is there really a lot of quicksand?" says Casey.

Goldwater nods. "When the river dries up, it's all over. You gotta be careful. My uncle knows where it is."

O-oh ti-eye-dings of cuh-umfort and joy.

·

Rock-blocked path twists and angles back on itself, drops drunkenly down, down into the depths of the Canyon de Chelley. Unsure footing. Careful now. One slip could end it all below on the packed red earth of the floor. Dusk approaches. Casey and Elise, all alone, explore.

White people aren't supposed to venture into the canyon without a Navajo guide. Not only is it against reservation statute, it violates local taboo, too. Could get shot. Stories go around. Unescorted Anglos unwelcome. Whose canyon is this, anyway? Not two weeks after Casey first arrived cops found a tourist with a bullet in his head, body all stiff, eyes staring, staring, and fingers clutching the pebbles at the base of Spider Rock in the obstinate close-mindedness of rigor mortis.

Who knows? Maybe Spider Woman shot him. Spider Rock's keeping the secret to itself. Shouldn't have been here in the first place, white man.

Yes, could be hazardous to the health. Elise says bullshit. She's walked the canyon before. She knows no fear, it seems. Wants to see nighttime clamp its star-strewn bowl tight over the rims of this chasm. Casey follows.

Who can see them at night, anyway?

Besides, Elise looks Navajo in the dark. She's got that long, straight black hair and a dark complexion and high cheekbones. She could pass for half-Navajo, at least, especially in the dark. Casey's the only one who looks white. Anyway, they're not tourists and they're exploring a more secluded section, the part where the canyon thins and finally becomes solid earth again. No one lives here. It's far from Spider Rock.

So why does Casey feel so uncomfortable?

Really, he feels like he'd be somehow more secure standing at the foot of Spider Rock itself, right there at the exact spot where the dead man stained the red sand with his white blood. Listening to the hoarse, breathy noises Spider Rock must make as it cuts the wind in thirds. Anybody comes at him with a gun, he could at least see where that somebody's coming from. Not like here where anybody or anything could be waiting behind a jut of rock.

So you see the person with the gun. So what? What do you do with this advantage? Say howdy, brother, peace, sister? Hey, I know you! You're a human being, right? What a coincidence, me too! Us human beings gotta stick together, right?

Bang-bang-you're-dead, right?

Reminds Casey of that time he had that summer job driving forklift for 7-Up. Got to be friendly with some of the black guys in the department. After-work drinking buddies. They didn't mind him being a honky, they told him, so long as he didn't *act* too much like a honky. Casey tried his best and soon enough he didn't feel too much like a honky at all. One day one of them—shipping clerk named Darnell Williams—invites Casey to a party in the Bronx. Southside, rough address. Casey jokes about how he doesn't know how safe he'll be, him being so white and walking those streets at night.

Darnell tears a scrap of cardboard from a shipping box, writes on it in big block letters, hands it to Casey.

THIS CARD ENTITLES THE BEARER
TO FREE PASSAGE
ANYWHERE IN THIS NEIGHBORHOOD

"Anybody fucks with you," says Darnell, "you show 'em this."

Turned out Casey never had to present the card at all. Just carrying it in his pocket was magic enough. Too bad nobody's given Casey the Canyon de Chelley card. Then he could check out Spider Rock anytime he wants to.

They reach the bottom. Elise leads the way. Orange sand in the twilight. Walls close in. Path narrows. Slice of deep blue above. Footsteps bounce back and forth against steep ripples of sandstone. They walk more softly.

"Sure is spooky," Casey says. He wonders how many times *that's* been said here. Canyon won't say.

But it *is* spooky here, with a kind of spookiness a haunted house—something merely man-made—could never match. Some portentous, prehistorical hoodoo could go on here. Canyon spirits could call on vital natural forces and Yeibichei Dancers could dance their dances and the Spider Woman could weave her web, cast it high from here and whirling wild and wanton round the world to catch up everything—and everything, *anything* would be possible, here, now.

Elise stumbles before him. He moves to catch her, but she regains her own balance. The path is only about a foot wide now. Dry desert bushes block the way every now and then, and Elise and Casey must scrabble their way up the steep walls to pass them.

The chilly air turns their breath to smoke.

They round a bend. Elise stops suddenly, gasps. Casey jumps forward, bumps past her.

There, inside a hollow pocket in the wall, posted on a pointed stick lodged firm in a crevasse, is the skull of a dog or coyote or something. Little bits of flesh and fur still cling to the bone. The skull is all abristle with long wooden needles.

Elise backs a step. "What… oh… Casey."

Casey breathes. "What *is* it?"

Elise says she doesn't know. Her voice trembles.

"God, it's ugly."

"It's getting too dark," says Elise. "I think we should go back."

And they make good time retracing their steps. And the air becomes colder and colder, almost as though a vacuum lay behind them, sucking up all of the canyon's heat. Neither of them turns around to check it out. And neither of them says a word until they reach the rim of the canyon and get in Casey's car and head for home. Then they can let loose nervous giggles and make fun of each other's fear and talk like it's no big deal. Just a Navajo no-trespassing sign.

And still, white man can't shake the feeling that he should have ripped the doghead thing from its secret nook and taken it with him. Who knows when such a thing might come in handy? Make a dandy conversation piece, if nothing else.

·

Elise lies asleep next to him. A soft breeze filters through the window screen. Air is stifling during the day, but beginning to cool come nightfall. Casey's turning over and over in bed. Can't sleep.

No lovemaking this evening. Elise's having her period, heavy flow, some cramps. She just doesn't feel like it, she says. Casey goes along. Can't sleep now, though. Keeps drifting off, but can't quite make it.

Having those crazy, wispy, half-awake, half-asleep dreams that start before you know it and end before they're finished.

Dusk. Casey walking the floor of the canyon. Walls rise high to either side, echo the dull rasp of footsteps in hard red sand. Looking up at the sky, catching sight of a monumental double spire breaking cleanly through the distance. Light of a crescent moon hangs low, polishes red sandstone, makes it gleam, dance, sparkle against a wallflower backdrop.

Coming closer.

Standing at the base. Looking up. So high it is. It reminds him of Manhattan.

Something standing on top of the tallest point. Stretching arms wide. It is the Spider Woman.

Casey wishes she would come down.

And suddenly a whooshing of wind in his ears, a whipping of things in his head, a whirling, a motion, a woman arcing down on a strand of moonlight to land warm, so warm, and real before him. She is clothed in a black web.

What is her name?

Touching him now, so warm, and now they are airborne and the night is all around and the stars are spinning and now they are atop the pinnacle and the woman is touching him and gazing deep, deep.

She looks like Elise. Only taller. Only darker.

She picks him up and he asks her what her name is.

She lays him down so softly. The web unraveling. He is stirred and asks for her name.

She mounts him and he feels her warmth and he is falling backwards, losing his hold in one great dizzying rush and still she is pressing forward and he is inside of her, shuddering, shuddering, and he turns over and puts his arm across Elise's back. She says something. He lifts his head.

"You awake?" he says.

No answer.

"You're taking all the covers," he complains.

Casey turns over on his back. His erection is a dull throb poking a peak in the sheet. Jesus! The thing won't rest easy for one lousy night. He'll be glad when Elise's period is over.

∙

Laundry day. Time for Casey to make himself useful. Earn his keep. Make Elise happy. Gather together all of their clothes and wash them free of Painted Desert. All by himself in a laundromat full of Navajo women. Stone faces. No one says nothing to nobody. Machines sudsing and whirring. Casey's clothes on spin dry and he just knows he'll take them home wet again. Plenty of washers in the place—Navajo women can't fill them all—but only half as many dryers.

Maybe he should ask somebody about a job here. Cleaning machines at night or something. He's tried everyplace else. Chinle's two gas stations. Chinle's one bank. The Chinle Cafeteria, Chinle Motel, and Chinle's one decent restaurant specializing in Mexican and Navajo food. Always the same response. Words are different, but that look they give you means the same in any language. Are you kidding? Whatever would we do with you?

Maybe some other time.

Navajo cowboys parked in their pickup trucks out the window, waiting for the clean duds.

Woman's work.

Casey always brings a book to read. Either that or stare at people who won't meet your eye for anything in the world. And they say New York's a cold city.

Cycle's almost over now. Casey glances across the room at the driers. All filled. It doesn't matter if he waits on line for one because Navajo women using the driers will take out their dry clothes and shove in their neighbor's wet clothes quicker than he can do anything about it. Block him right out. And what's he going to do about it anyway? Create a scene? Demand his rights? Freeze, lady, I was here first. Oh, no. The *bilagáana* have only as much right as they will take, and they've taken those rights over and over again.

But not Casey. No. Not *this* white man.

The washer spins to a stop and Casey pulls the damp clothes out, glances once more at the driers, throws the clothes in the basket and carries them out the door to his car. He can hang them up to dry at home. They'll collect some red dust in the creases and corners, but then again, what doesn't?

•

Chill air braces the nostrils. Light covering of snow climbs the ragged incline, becomes quickly skidmarked and muddy from the small-soled boots of twenty Navajo children. Four cars full of Elise's students tramping up the slope to find that perfect Christmas tree for the classroom. Everybody's saying this one! this one! Elise's far behind talking with good old Captain Hook who's helping with the driving. Wouldn't you know. Casey hasn't seen him much since that first time they met. He drops by every now and then. Doesn't say much to Casey. Doesn't stay long. Maybe Casey really did give him a bad first impression. He certainly seems to be avoiding Casey as much as he can today.

No loss.

Quite the class excursion. Everybody having a good time. Casey's well ahead of the pack with this kid Goldwater. Scouting. Elise tells him that Goldwater's supposed to be some kind of bad-ass, so watch out for him, but as far as Casey can tell, he's a good kid. Quiet, yes, but he doesn't look like trouble. He's been sticking close to Casey since they left Chinle. Sat right next to him on the ride up. Hung near by his side when they organized the kids arriving in the other three cars. Casey's getting to enjoy the kid's company. Beats the hell out of listening to the rest of those kids jabber and giggle.

Scouting the higher ground. Trees at the bottom look too scrawny for Casey's taste. Goldwater carries the hatchet. Casey carries the ticket that cost three dollars out of the class treasury that allows them one tree on this reservation-regulated hill.

The blue and white peaks of the Lukachukai Mountains rise before them.

"God, it's good to get out of Chinle," says Casey. "It's beautiful up here."

Goldwater says nothing. He's checking out trees.

And then they come to it. The one. The only tree there is. Twice Casey's height it stands. Full with branches upraised to the sky. They stand alone for a while. Staring. The branches grab the breeze, toss sprinkles of snow in their faces. Casey whistles.

"This one," says Goldwater, finally.

Casey stirs. "It's almost a shame to cut it down, it looks so good."

Goldwater nods, smiles, points to some smaller, adjacent trees. "These gotta have a chance to grow, too," he says.

And he looks straight up into Casey's face, eye meeting eye, and smiles such a warm, friendly smile. Suddenly—who knows why?—Casey feels really good. God*damn* good! His heart soars higher than a cloud. He squats on his haunches—eye level, now—and musses Goldwater's hair roughly.

"What the hell do you know about trees?" he says, laughing. "You're just a Chinle city boy."

And Goldwater ducks his head and laughs with him and—yes, it's true, Indians can do it—blushes and finally pulls away and begins attacking the base of the tree with the little hand axe. Casey gets a kick out of this. He figures it'll take the kid all day to chop down that big tree with that puny hatchet.

"Goldwater, maybe we better wait for the others."

"Fuck 'em," Goldwater grunts, still swinging. "This is the one we want."

And then it happens. Captain Hook. Crashing through the trees. Slipping in the snow. Tangling in the underbrush. Stumbling past Casey and grabbing Goldwater and pulling him up by one arm.

"Hey! Hey, what are you doing?" he's saying. "We only get one tree. They picked it out already down below."

Goldwater squirms away from the grip, bends, starts chopping again.

Hook pulls him up again. "Listen, boy—"

Goldwater menaces him with the hatchet.

Casey steps forward, mouth open.

Hook catches Goldwater's free hand, wrenches the hatchet away, throws it behind him. "You little motherfucker," he hisses and picks Goldwater off the ground by his coat front. Goldwater struggles and kicks fiercely.

Something must be done.

"Put him down," says Casey.

Maybe it's his tone of voice, or maybe the Captain's arms are getting tired. No easy trick holding a wild savage in mid-air. Hook puts him down. Goldwater runs behind the tree.

Hook waves his arms. "That little son of a bitch—"

"Shut up!" Casey snarls.

Hook's face is a red blotch. He sputters and bubbles like a stewed tomato. Casey tries to think. No need for any scenes here. Instinct says one thing. Reason another. The Captain is big, all right. Two or three inches taller and a good twenty pounds heavier. Of course, a lot of that's fat, but never underestimate the power of fat. Hook's got the high ground, too. Smart thing to do is tidy everything up nice and polite and friendly. Two points of view in every disagreement. Oh, but Goldwater's watching the scene from behind a screen of pine needles, and Casey knows that if there's one thing at all that he and this Navajo boy will ever have in common, it's that neither of them ever want to listen to anything the Captain has to say.

Little voices sing far down the hill.

"Apologize to Goldwater," says Casey.

"Jesus Christ, I don't see—"

"Apologize."

"Well, Jesus, I didn't mean to hurt him—I'm sorry if I did—but that little—"

"If you ever," says Casey slowly, "*ever* touch that kid again, I'll fucking kill you."

Hook falters. "Are you crazy?"

"Do you understand what I'm telling you?"

"Sure, you don't have to—"

"Then get the fuck out of here right now."

Hook hesitates, says what the hell, walks around Casey and down the hill. Goldwater comes out from behind the tree, looks up at Casey from beneath lowered lids.

"Come on, Goldwater. Grab the axe. We'll go down and tell them we have the tree up here. We'll take a vote on which one they want."

And Goldwater follows Casey down the slope and they gather the others and bring them up and the class decides that, indeed, the higher tree is the only tree. And Goldwater goes on cutting it down all by himself.

And Elise asks Casey what the hell happened between Roger and him.

"Where is he?" says Casey.

"He went back to his car. He seemed pretty upset. He says you're crazy."

Casey smiles. "He's an asshole."

Elise doesn't like that. "Listen," she says, "Roger's doing me a big favor helping today. We couldn't have done this without him. He drove seven kids in his car."

"Let him tend to the kids in *his* car, then, and leave my kids the fuck alone!"

Elise's eyebrows arch. "*Your* kids?"

Casey doesn't answer.

"Hey, what does Goldwater have to do with this?"

"Nothing," says Casey.

"What happened with you and Roger?"

Casey says he'll tell her later, he doesn't feel like discussing it right now.

"Listen, it's nice that you're playing big brother and everything," says Elise, "but don't act like a jerk."

And Casey watches the tree fall, smiling to himself.

·

Swinging into the muddy, rutted drive. One lonely house trailer out in the middle of nowhere. About five miles outside Chinle. Still nowhere. Small area around the trailer enclosed by a rusty wire fence. What the hell are they keeping out? Certainly not the desert. Wheels slipping in deep puddles, spraying jets of mud in their wake.

Casey stops at the gate. Gets out. Opens Belladonna's door. "I'll take her in," says Elise.

Dog tied up next to the trailer beginning to whine. Elise and Belladonna go through the gate, enter the trailer. Casey walks around the back of the car, checks the rope that secures the tree to the open tailgate. Car door slams. Goldwater stands next to him.

"Holding pretty good," says Casey.

Goldwater nods.

Casey leans on the side of the car, slaps his shirt pockets for a cigarette. Goldwater taps his arm, holds the pack out.

Casey takes it. He lights one.

"Gimme a cigarette," says Goldwater.

"Can't do it. Nasty habit. Make you die young."

Just like Casey's father told him back in the good old days, puffing on a Camel. What is it about kids that makes you feel old all of a sudden? Casey takes a deep drag, blows smoke into the gray mist. God, it's an ugly day down here. Good day to be out of Chinle. Rainy season's giving him the blues. Nothing for the rain to do here. No grass to make greener. No flowers to bloom. May as well snow. Should have stayed in the mountains. At least they have trees. Elise says these kids hardly ever get out of Chinle. Never see real houses. Never run in real grass. Just dust and desert, all the time. Depressing.

Elise says she tries to tell them how important it is to be educated. Kids want to know why. Elise says, well, so they can make a living if they decide to go off the reservation someday. Go off the reservation? What for? It's really sad, Elise says. What they don't know. What they don't want to know. What they're afraid of knowing.

"You like getting out of Chinle?" Casey says.

Goldwater says he doesn't mind.

"You ever go off the reservation?"

"Been to Gallup," says Goldwater.

"I mean *really* off. You ever been to Phoenix?"

Goldwater shakes his head.

"Me neither. Elise says it's really nice. Maybe sometime we could take a trip there. You know, if it's okay with your father." Casey hesitates. "I mean, if you'd like to sometime. It'd be good for you to take a trip, you know?"

Goldwater looks at the ground, looks up into Casey's eyes. "Let me have a cigarette," he says. "Just one."

Casey shakes his head, laughs. What the hell? He pulls the pack from his pocket, takes out two cigarettes. "Put them away for now," he says. "And don't tell Elise I gave you any. She won't like it."

Goldwater puts them in his jacket pocket.

"Hey," says Casey. "I been wondering. How'd you get your name? I mean, does it have any special meaning?"

Goldwater shrugs. "My father gave it to me."

"It doesn't mean anything special?"

Goldwater looks away. "Is it supposed to?"

Dumbass question anyway. Of course. Still. "Casey's not my real name," says Casey. "My real name's Kenneth Cory."

Goldwater smiles at the ground. "What's that supposed to mean?"

"Nothing," Casey chuckles. "I mean, my father's name was Kenneth Cory, too. They always called me by my initials. K.C. Casey. Get it?"

Goldwater nods. He's looking off into the sky. Casey lays his hand on his shoulder. Goldwater stands still.

And Elise's coming out of the trailer now and through the gate. Goldwater gets back in the front seat through Casey's door. Casey opens the back door for Elise.

"Jesus," she whispers. "You should see what a dump that place is."

•

Saturday morning in Gallup. Ugly town. Railroad tracks. Hot, sun-savaged streets lined with bars. Houses off somewhere away from the tumble and confusion of downtown. Up on the heights somewhere. Houses, yes, but strangely box-like. Two-story immobile mobile homes. No grass. No trees. No front porch on a Saturday morning.

Casey and Elise walking downtown. Seeing the sights. Hitting the liquor store. Maybe catch a movie this afternoon.

Streets are crowded. Seems like the whole reservation has the same idea. Storefronts are blocked by an endless line of Navajo cowboys. Waiting for the bars to open. Or camped out from a reckless Friday night. Who knows? Casey doesn't ask. White man minds his own business, walks past it all, glances neither to the left nor the right, talks with Elise about nothing. Talking gives him a purpose on these streets.

And now a voice behind them.

"Brother, hey!"

Louder and nearer. Casey minding his own business before him. A hand on his shoulder. Elise stops two steps ahead, curious.

Casey turns around to see a short, grey-headed, bleary-eyed black man. The first he's seen in these parts.

"You gotta smoke, brother?"

Casey says sure, pulls one out. Black man's weaving back and around like the earth's spinning too fast for him. Heavy lidded eyes wrinkle at the corners. Yellow teeth shine in the sun. Gums are bleeding. Black man tries once, catches the cigarette on his second grab. Makes humming, clucking noises in his throat.

"Gotta light?"

Casey pulls out a Bic, follows the end of the cigarette around a few figure eights, finally gets it going.

"Thank *you*, m'man."

And Casey's turning away.

"Hey, hey! Wait a minute, brother."

"Yeah?"

"You got some spare money?"

Casey laughs. "You know anybody's got spare money? I ain't got shit."

Black man's talking fast and slurry. "Hey, baby, listen, listen! You ain't from *around* here."

Casey says no.

"You from the east, hey? Where you from?"

"New York," says Casey. "City."

Black man's reeling and swinging his arms out, brushing into some people passing by. "Shit, me either. I'm from *Cleve*land! Practically your back yard."

Elise tugs on Casey's arm. "Come on," she says.

Casey turns.

Blank, burnt brown, heavy-cheeked faces grow from the storefront, rest atop shoulders hunched by folded arms. Red, craggy faces topped by black hair and white cowboy hats. Tightly muscled faces full of squinted black eyes, staring, staring. What are they looking at? He should be walking, breaking each line of vision only for the barest of moments. Like a wink.

"Come *on*, Casey."

Sun is so hot. He shouldn't stand still in the sun. Surrounding air picks up the body heat, chokes the brain.

"Hey brother, you hear what I'm sayin'? What you doin' way the hell an' gone in this motherfucker?"

Keep moving and the body heat dissipates, gets new air to suck it up. But these Navajos don't know this. Stand in the sun all day and never *think* of moving.

A hand on his arm. He flinches. He looks. It's black. It's attached to a short body. On the body rests wagging— threatening now to fall off—a grey and black head with a red and yellow mouth that is moving, moving. "Brothers gotta stick together. Red man don't give a shit 'bout us. No credit. That's all. Been livin' here ten motherfuckin' *years*! Just a *taste*! All I want. Man's 'bout to shake his ass through the floor this mornin'. No motherfuckin' credit."

Yellow eyes, all bloodshot and milky and open wide and fiery. "Hey! You know what I'm talkin'? Baby, we's all we got. Red man don't give a shit, you know?"

"I know," says Casey. He glances over his shoulder. Elise's twenty feet up the street, weight resting on one leg, arms folded, staring. The storefront line-up is staring like a row of mannequins, or—he hates to think of it—cigar store Indians.

He starts to draw away. Hand on his arm again.

"Hey, I speaks their lingo." Yellow grin. Head tilted back. "Tha's right. Fucks 'em up, too, me talkin' their shit. You don't believe it?"

The black man backs up a step and begins to speak loudly in what very well may be Navajo. It's difficult for Casey to tell for sure. He doesn't recognize Navajo words. He can only identify the Navajo tongue by its tone. Navajo spoken in black accent could be pure gibberish, as far as he knows. But the black man is talking louder and louder and Casey is afraid that he may be saying something insulting to the Navajo race, though no one passing by, no one standing to the side pays any attention.

Casey backs, turns, walks quickly away. The gibberish stops.

"Hey, brother, hey!" he hears behind him, but he's caught up with Elise now and they continue their walk and he doesn't look back.

"Jesus Christ!" says Elise. "Do you have to stop and talk to every junkie on the street? That guy was disgusting."

"He was talking to me," Casey says. "I couldn't just walk away."

"Why not? He couldn't stand up straight, he couldn't even *talk* straight, and you have to carry on a conversation like he's an old army buddy or something. Since when are you so goddamn polite?"

"I don't know. I kind of felt sorry for him."

Elise sighs, shakes her head. "Well, at least you didn't give him money," she says.

•

Wintertime's here. Hasn't snowed yet. Nothing but this lousy, cold rain. But winter's definitely here. And it's killing him slow.

Holidays in New York would be nice. See the family. Check out Central Park. Real, live grass underfoot, even if it's dying of the cold. Real buildings taller than one story. Houses. No more trailers. No more red dust and mud. Things to do. Catch a concert. See a show. No Saturday night in Chinle sitting in the trailer getting loaded.

Something. Something different. Something the same.

Casey tells Elise he could use a break.

"I know," she says. "This place can get to you sometimes."

"I like it here and everything. I mean, the country around here is really gorgeous. It just gets kind of boring. God, I miss walking to the corner bar for a drink. I miss walking on a real paved street."

Elise does too.

"I miss trees," says Casey. "Like maple trees and oak trees. And tree lawns."

Elise pours them each another drink.

"I'd like to be in New York for the holidays," Casey says.

"Me too," says Elise. "I don't think I can afford it, though."

"I'm thinking of going."

Elise nods. "It would probably be good for you. Can you afford the plane fare?"

"I'd have to take my car."

"Will it make it?"

"It'll have to."

A pause follows. Elise stares at Casey, eyes narrowing. "You're not talking about coming back, are you?"

"Elise, if I go…" He hesitates. "I don't think so. There's no way I can afford to. I'm down to practically no money. I'll have to get a job as soon as I get back to the city, just to live."

Elise takes a sip of her drink, stares into the glass. "Stay with me."

"I don't know if I can afford to, Elise. I've been here three months now, and it doesn't look like I'll ever get a job. And I can't keep living off of you."

Elise says that she's never complained. Let her worry about that.

"Baby, I may go *crazy* here."

"You'll go crazy in the city, too. You'll get sick of that quick enough."

Casey knows. He knows.

"Let's go for a walk," says Elise.

They take their drinks with them and walk to the edge of the trailer compound and climb the hill that Casey has never been able to figure out. It looks like a natural formation, but also it looks like somebody put it there with about a thousand dump trucks to remind everybody that Chinle was once a place of great geological upheaval. They get to the top. And there are just so many stars. No skies like this back east. There's almost too many of them. Casey couldn't pick out a separate constellation if he tried. He doesn't. He simply stares upwards, lost in the chaos of scattered lights.

"Do you want to leave me?" says Elise.

"I don't want to leave you. I just want to leave this place. It's too—too big, I guess."

That's not it, Casey knows. But what it is, he doesn't know. Words are so useless.

"I feel very lonely here sometimes," he says.

That's not it either.

"Elise, I think maybe I just don't belong here."

This may be it, but it's just too, too corny if it is.

Elise puts down her drink—the unlevel earth spills it— and puts her arms around Casey's neck and hugs him so goddamn tight that she almost pulls him over. He feels dizzy for a moment. Gets a light-headed feeling like he's slipping, floating off the top of the hill.

"You'll be lonely in New York," she says. "You'll wish you were here with me."

Highly possible. Probable, even. What brought him way the hell out into this goddamn desert in the first place?

"Listen, I'm sure you'll be able to get a job after Christmas. The guy in charge of food service says they always have a lot of openings after Christmastime. A lot of people quit then."

"And they always replace them with Navajos."

"I'll talk to him. You'll get a job."

Casey says nothing.

"We can go someplace else for the holidays."

Casey gently disengages himself, takes the last sip of his drink.

"We can go to Phoenix. It's really nice there. We can stay in a nice hotel with a swimming pool and a big lawn with palm trees."

Casey laughs softly.

Elise smiles. "We can walk downtown at night and look at all the lights and eat in restaurants and ride elevators up to the tops of the tallest buildings. And we can go to the zoo and see the animals play all day long. Casey, we can do all kinds of good things."

Casey feels giddy. "Can we sit out on the veranda of a Mexican restaurant and drink Margaritas and watch all the people walk by?"

"Of course we can! And you'll feel right at home, too. There's more New Yorkers in Phoenix than there are in New York."

"I don't know," says Casey. "Can we not think about Chinle at all, and not talk about it?"

Elise nods, and she kisses him so sweetly.

"I don't know. I really don't know what I should do."

"Do what I tell you," says Elise, and she laughs because it is so apparent that she and inertia have Casey where he is, and everything is fine now. And they walk slowly down the hill, arm in arm, falling and giggling like a couple of drunken maniacs, and leaving the stars shining on the Navajo Nation above and behind them.

•

Dropping off Goldwater. Last kid to go. Driving into the low-rent compound and off a side road. Stopping in front of a corrugated metal and left-over aluminum siding shack. Casey half expects to see a big, ugly, drunken Indian around somewhere. Nothing happening, though.

Elise opens the door. "Do you want me to take you in?" she says. "Tell your father why we're late?"

Goldwater glances at Casey, says no, gets out.

"Why don't you thank Casey for the ride?" says Elise.

Goldwater makes a certain noise.

Casey says that's all right, he doesn't need any thank-yous, thank you. Elise says these kids have to learn some manners *some*time. Casey smiles, says not on my watch. Goldwater turns his back, hunches his shoulders, turns around to face the car with a big, smug grin and a lit cigarette sticking out of his face.

Casey shakes his head. He has to laugh. He really does.

"Casey, he stole one of your cigarettes."

Casey waves goodbye, turns the car around.

"Casey!"

"I gave it to him," says Casey. "It won't kill him."

"Goddamnit, Casey, I *asked* you not to give him a cigarette, didn't I?"

Casey doesn't remember that specific request.

"Jesus, I can't believe you. These are *my* students. I'm responsible for them. If his father catches him and complains to the school—"

"His father won't give a shit."

Elise stares straight ahead. "Just don't give shit to my students, okay?"

"Oh, come on, Elise. He kept asking and asking me. I had to give him one."

"You don't *have* to do *anything*," Elise says, voice all cold and low. "You always just do what you want to do."

Well. What the hell? Casey's sorry, anyway. He pulls onto the main road, heads for the school, starts to whistle a Christmas carol. I'll be home for Christmas. You can count on me. Elise looks out the side window. What for? Landscape's looking fairly bleak.

"You know," Casey says casually. "Goldwater's not a bad kid."
"I know."

"I told him I'd take him to Phoenix sometime. You think it's a good idea? It'd get him out of Chinle."

"Great," says Elise. "We can take him for the holidays. A week of you and Goldwater would be such a nice vacation."

Oh, oh, oh. Been a long day for Elise, it seems. Feeling somewhat touchy.

"I don't know about you," says Casey, "but I had a pretty good time today. I like playing with the kids, you know?"

"Wonderful."

Casey's jaw works. "Listen, I had a good time, all right? Just because you're tired, you don't have to spoil *my* day."

Elise shakes her head slowly, eyes wide. "Huh!" she says, finally. "Yeah, I certainly don't want to spoil your day. I mean, just because Roger's all pissed off about some silly thing or other and won't talk to me, just because Goldwater smokes one of your cigarettes right in front of his teacher, just because I sing my little heart out all the way back and you encourage the boys to think it's *stupid*—"

"I didn't encourage anybody."

"No, of course not. Elise's just tired, that's all. I'm glad you had a good time. I'm glad you're so good with the kids." Elise snorts. "You act just like one."

Casey runs both of his hands through his hair. The car steers itself for a moment. "I didn't realize I was acting like a kid."

"You probably weren't," says Elise. "Acting, I mean."

It wasn't like that, Casey knows. Really, he felt good today. He felt like he was *doing* something. He clears his throat. "Let's just not talk about this now, okay? I don't feel like fighting about anything."

Elise says that's fine with her, she just feels like having a drink and taking it easy, so they should unload this fucking tree and get home.

Up ahead, the road winds on to follow the length of the canyon. Casey turns into the school grounds. Night is beginning to fall. He'll have to apologize to Elise later tonight. After a couple drinks and a joint. They'll both feel better then. Really, there's no sense fighting with Elise. No sense at all.

EVERY GODDAMN THING

Goddamn Cat

The problem was her cat. I was against getting it in the first place but all of a sudden my wife's a goddamn feline freak so she got her way as usual. Goddamn unlucky black cat too, not that I'm superstitious, all sneaky and alien-eyed, shedding fleas all over the goddamn house and arching its stupid back and rubbing up against my leg when I least expected it, like the night I went to the fridge for another beer and it dodged underfoot and I tripped and damn near broke my neck.

Well, I grabbed that god*damn* squirmy cat and the thing raked me three bloody tracks from crook of elbow to wrist. "Goddamn!" I yelled and I heaved it out the back door hard as I could. Goddamn cat hit the ground and took off for the palmetto bushes where it cried like a baby and woke up my wife.

So I was in the bathroom cursing up a storm, looking for some goddamn gauze or band-aids or something, when my wife came in all bleary-eyed and irritable.

"What is *with* you?" she screamed. "What is your *prob*lem?"

"Your goddamn cat is my goddamn problem. I'm about to kill that scrawny bastard."

That's when she went off again, telling me how maybe *I* was the goddamn problem: I drink too much, I'm lazy, I can't control my temper, all I'm good for is laying on the sofa in front of the boob tube emptying beer cans and filling up ashtrays blah-blah-blah, same old shit.

Meantime blood was oozing from these deep scratches. I dabbed at them with a wad of wet toilet paper. "I'm good for a paycheck every week, I guess," I said.

She kind of snorted. "Not much of one."

"More than yours."

"Not much more."

She had on that old dumpy flannel nightgown she always wore, even in the summer. Her face was all puffy and her hair was matted on one side and frizzed out on the other. She wasn't exactly a vision of loveliness, I'll tell you, and I had a hard time looking at her.

"Hey, we got any goddamn Bactine or anything?" I said.

She sighed and bumped me out of the way with her hip and pulled a bottle of rubbing alcohol from the cupboard below the sink. "Use this," she said.

"That'll sting like shit."

She shrugged. "I hope you're not looking for sympathy."

As a matter of fact, I wouldn't have minded some. Jesus, I was hurt. Where was the goddamn love? I stuck my arm in the sink, grabbed the bottle and poured it all over those goddamn scratches. My vision blurred purple and I cursed between clenched teeth. I snatched a face towel off the rack and blotted at the blood and alcohol.

"Not with my good towel!" she yelled.

"Fuck your towel."

She stood there all rigid, jaw working, and then she started in again about how worthless I was. I was supposed to paint the house two months ago—she bought me the paint and everything. She asked me to change the oil in her Honda last month and she ended up just going to Jiffy-Lube. And what about that broken hinge on the kitchen cupboard? How long was I going to let it just hang there from a twist tie?

"I'll get around to it. We got any gauze? I'm bleeding to death here."

"You'll get around to it," she said. "Right. You haven't even gotten around to mowing the lawn in the last three weeks."

"Lawnmower's broke."

"Then fix it."

I couldn't find any gauze or tape or anything so I just wrapped that goddamn towel around my arm and fastened it with a rubber band I found in the back of a drawer. I pushed past her out of the bathroom, pretty pissed off at this point.

"Why don't you get your handyman boyfriend to fix it," I said.

She looked at me, eyes turning to slits. "What did you say?"

"You heard me. Get old lover-boy Tom to fix it. He's good with his hands, ain't he?" I looked away but it was too late to stop. "As long as he's fucking my wife, he can at least fix my goddamn mower."

She looked shook up at first but then she folded her arms and glared at me. "Have you completely lost it?" she said. "Have you finally just totally lost your fucking mind?"

"I know what I know," I said.

My arm stung like crazy. I went to the kitchen, pulled a bottle of Jim Beam from the cupboard and gulped down a swig. She was right there behind me.

"You don't know shit," she said. "Have another drink, why don't you. That'll make you smarter."

I peeled back the bloody towel from my arm. The scratches were ugly, all puffed up and angry and oozing. "I know I never should've let you buy that goddamn cat!" I said. "I oughta get my gun and shoot its ass right now!"

And that's when she hit me over the head with a dirty pot from the sink. I went down on one knee. I looked up, half blind with pain, and she was standing there crying. The pot clanged on the linoleum. "That cat has a goddamn name, you know!" She stormed away to the bedroom.

I got to my feet, stumbled to the fridge, and got myself a beer. I held the can against my throbbing head for a minute before I popped it and chugged it down. By that time I could hear her wrestling our suitcase from the closet. I popped open another beer. "Cheers," I said.

Goddamn Wife

She didn't take the goddamn cat with her. It was still hanging around the neighborhood. I'd be damned if I could remember its goddamn name. Damned if I gave a shit.

Two nights after she left I heard it yowling outside. I opened the window wide and yelled at it to shut the fuck up. I thought I saw a pair of eyes glowing from the palmetto bushes, and if I had my gun I would've shot the goddamn thing right between them. But my wife packed my gun when she left. That and her clothes. I found out later, when I was looking for our homeowner's policy, she took her birth certificate too. The goddamn cat shut up and I closed the window. I guess I missed my goddamn wife a little—I hadn't had sex since two weeks before she left—but I also enjoyed having that king-size bed all to myself. I took a sip of Jim Beam from the bottle on the nightstand and I sprawled all across that bed, my side and hers.

I figured she'd come back soon enough—she had no family to go to—but later in the week when I called the shop at the mall where she worked the girl who answered said my wife had quit. "Didn't you know?" she said, her voice sweet as gossip syrup.

"The husband's always the last to know," I said and hung up.

I checked at the bank and learned she took half of the savings—a little less than a thousand—so I figured she wouldn't last long. But the truth is I wasn't in any hurry to see her come back. We'd married out of high school and we'd been fighting pretty regular the twelve years since. I'm not saying we didn't have our good times. We used to party till we couldn't stand up straight and she was a lot of fun in bed at the start, I'll give her that. But none of those good times ever turned into good memories. They just weren't real clear in my mind. All we did anymore was fight or ignore each other. The year before I'd got kind of desperate and told her maybe we should think about having a kid or something but she just shook her head and laughed and a little later she bought that goddamn cat and started spoiling it rotten.

I should've known then it was all over.

Goddamn House

The goddamn house was in as good a shape as the goddamn marriage. Everything was falling apart. Cheap-ass cinderblock and plywood construction. Roof leaked over the carport and those rafters were rotting out. Circuit breakers tripped when my wife turned on the vacuum while the dishwasher was running. Linoleum peeled up in the kitchen and wallpaper unfurled in the living room. Pump for my irrigation well broke down last spring and now the only green in the lawn was the weeds. Before she left I'd sometimes have a beer out in the hammock in the back yard. I'd look at the loose roof shingles and the hairline cracks in the cinderblocks running down to the foundation, and I'd listen to the windows rattle in their cheap-ass casements every time a plane came in low for the airport south of us, and I'd pray for a hurricane to roll through so I could collect the insurance and leave the rubble behind.

But if I thought things were falling apart before my wife left, everything really started going to hell after. First the compressor on the fridge went, so I ate at McDonald's and bought a bag of ice and a 12-pack for the cooler every day after work. Then the garbage disposal went so I quit using the kitchen sink. Then lightning zapped my 52-inch TV in the family room—that's when I looked for the homeowner's policy but it had a $500 deductible—so I hauled the cooler to the bedroom and watched the little 13-incher. Then the AC started acting up, the blower running 24/7 but the air barely cooler than outside. I opened up the air handler and brushed about a ton of dust from the coils and that seemed to help but the compressor was still laboring.

That first month without her was a regular planned obsolescence curse.

Then the bearings went on the dryer drum and it ground to a halt right in the middle of a load of my work uniforms. I kicked it. I kicked it again. I kicked it and kicked it till I caved in the sheet metal and my foot hurt so bad I wanted to cry. But I didn't. I just hung my soggy uniforms to dry on every doorknob in the house and after that took my business to the laundromat.

Now all this time things were breaking down, I couldn't stop thinking about my neighbor Tom. He was 45 or so, never married, lived next door all these years taking care of his sick old mother who ended up dying a couple years back. Worked as maintenance foreman for a little plastic molding plant nearby. Nice looking guy with buzz-cut grey hair, shorter than me but pretty buff. You could tell he worked out. I'm saying it wasn't a stretch figuring what my wife saw in him—after the fact, of course. Before the fact, me and Tom got along pretty good. Thing is, this guy was handy. He could fix anything. If anything broke down around the house—weed whacker, toilet, car, even my CD player one time—all I had to do was take it to my carport with a six-pack of cold long necks and start tinkering with it and scratching my head. Pretty soon old Tom'd see me through his window and he'd be over in a flash with his tool case.

"Let me take a look at that thing, Gary," he'd say and I'd give him a beer, step back, and watch him go to work. By the time he finished the six-pack he'd usually have it fixed.

I'd caught them last winter when I came home from work early on my wife's day off, hoping for a little afternoon delight myself if you want to know the truth. The carport door to the house was locked. So was the front door. I rang the bell and when my wife didn't answer I fished my keys out of my pocket and opened the door. There she was on her way to the door all breathless, like I'd just woken her up or something. And there standing in the middle of the living room trying to look casual was Tom. He had his hands clasped behind him like a soldier at parade rest. Then he put his hands in his pockets and started jingling some change there. Then he clasped his hands in front of his crotch. He gave a lame smile.

"Hey, Gary," he said.

"You're home early," my wife said, trying her best to sound happy with that. "I didn't hear you drive in."

"Did you hear me ring the goddamn bell?"

"I was just coming to get it."

Tom hitched at his belt. His face was red. "I just dropped by to take a look at your circuit breakers," he said. "I really oughta rewire that board for you."

"You off work today?"

"I called in sick," he said. "I better go." He covered his mouth with his hand and gave this lame little breathless cough. "Don't want you catching this."

After Tom left, my goddamn wife touched my shoulder and opened her mouth to say something but I turned away. So she pretended she had important stuff going on in the kitchen and off she went. I never said a word about it—not until the night the goddamn cat scratched me. Tom quit stopping over. I'd see him now and again going or coming from work and he'd wave, but that was it.

In a way, that pissed me off more than anything. Here the goddamn house was coming apart at the seams and my goddamn wife had ruined my free handyman service for me.

Goddamn Job

I worked for Rid-a-Bug Exterminators spraying baseboards, attics, and crawl spaces and at the end of the day it took a six-pack just to wash out the taste of pesticide. I'd had the job for three years now and was doing pretty good up until the time my wife left. After that, I'll admit, I started hitting the bottle heavier than normal so I had to call in a day or two with the flu that first week. Then the next week my arm swelled up and started leaking stinking pus and hurt so bad I could barely move it, so I had to call in sick for real. I took a trip to the local doc-in-a-box where a physician's assistant shot me up with antibiotics, tetanus, and epinephrine and told me I was lucky I still had an arm. I lost four days of work that week plus the doc bill, and when I went back in the boss looked at me funny and asked if everything was okay at home.

I told him everything couldn't be better.

Then I missed a few more days of work over the next month and came in late a few more times and my boss started giving me a little hell but nothing major. Then end of August, two months after my wife left, I came in ten minutes late and the boss called me into his office. I was a little hung over and I started sweating as soon as he told me to take a seat. He was a big old bald guy with a big chest and no neck and right off he loosened his tie. He stared down at this manila file folder on his desk, bushy eyebrows furrowed.

"You like your job, Eppes?" he said.

The truth is it was a nowhere job and the pay sucked and I'd probably get cancer from the bug spray one of these days, but I told him I liked it just fine.

"Well, you don't act like it," he said. I opened my mouth to say something, but he put up his big palm to shut me up and he looked at the folder again and started listing all the days I'd called in sick or come in late over the past couple of months. "But that's not the worst of it," he said and looked straight at me. Even though his voice was gruff and no-nonsense his eyes looked kind of sad, like maybe he didn't particularly like his own job. "We got a complaint yesterday from a Mrs…" He ran his finger down a sheet of paper in the folder. "…a Mrs. Murphy. She says you came to her house drunk yesterday."

"I wasn't drunk," I said.

"Were you drinking?"

I didn't answer.

"She also says you got fresh with her."

"What?"

"Overly familiar. She says you propositioned her."

"Oh, hell, I asked her out is all."

"You asked out a married client of this company?"

I felt my face turning red. "I was just fooling around. She's always flirting with me. I just dished back what she dishes out all the time. She tell you how she pinched my ass when I was bent over spraying inside the air register?"

"I don't want to hear it," the boss interrupted. "I could fire your ass right now, Eppes." He sighed, ran a hand over his shiny dome. "Probably should and save us both the grief later. But I know you're having trouble at home—"

"Who told you that?"

"Doesn't matter. It's the only reason I'm giving you another chance. Get your shit together, Eppes. You call in sick or come in late or go to a house smelling of booze one more time and you're fired. Understood?"

"Yes sir," I said and then I thanked him and left for that day's route.

I didn't touch a drop from the pint of Jim Beam in the glove box of my truck all day, but by the time I got home I was itching for a drink. When I turned off the ignition the engine kept knocking and dieseling like it'd been doing for the past couple of weeks, so I mashed on the gas pedal till it died out. I grabbed the pint from the glove box, took a long swig, then got out of the truck.

"Evening, Gary," I heard behind me.

I turned. He was standing on his porch, hands in his pockets. "Hey, Tom," I said.

He nodded at my truck. "That sure doesn't sound good."

"Nope."

"Want me to take a look at it?"

"Maybe sometime." I looked down at the bottle in my hand and shrugged. "I'm kind of busy right now."

"Sure thing," Tom said. "See you later."

"See you later," I said and let myself in the house.

I polished off that pint and made my way through half of my nightstand bottle before I passed out. When I woke up the alarm radio had been blaring for forty minutes. I jumped out of bed, gulped down four aspirin with a big glass of water, and fought the urge to throw up while I got dressed. My head was spinning and I needed a cup of coffee bad but I headed straight to my truck. If I really booked I'd still make it to work on time.

Goddamn Truck

I hate to tell you but the story doesn't get much prettier at this point.

Talk about the worst time for things to fall apart, my goddamn truck wouldn't start. I kept cranking the ignition and pumping the gas, but the goddamn thing just wouldn't turn over. I looked at my watch. I tried again. All I was doing was wearing down the battery. I gave up and slumped forward till my head hit the steering column. The horn blared and I jumped. I pounded on the horn some more.

I was losing it.

I popped the hood and looked at the engine. I didn't know the first thing about fixing it. Nobody ever taught me shit. I stood there staring and cursing.

Then I heard Tom's door slam. I looked over and he was on his porch.

"Let me get my tools," he said.

In a couple of minutes he was under the hood and had the manifold off. I was telling him how I couldn't be late again, how my boss said I'd be fired if I was. My voice was shaking and cracking like I was a little kid ready to start bawling. Tom put a hand on my shoulder, squeezed it once, said he'd get this baby fired up pronto.

"I'm sure glad you were around, Tom," I said and then I didn't know what else to say. "Hey," I said. "Can I get you a beer?"

Tom laughed. He was leaning into the engine with a screwdriver. "I gotta go to work this morning too," he said. "I guess you didn't know I joined Alcoholics Anonymous."

"No," I said. "What for?"

"Because I'm an alcoholic, I guess."

"I never knew you had a drinking problem."

"I never knew it either. That's part of the problem." His eyes shifted to me then back to the engine. "Maybe you want to come to a meeting with me sometime," he said.

"You think I got a problem?"

"Doesn't matter what I think. The question is do *you* think so."

I studied this awhile. "I don't know," I said finally. "I'm not much of a joiner."

Tom nodded. "Standing invitation," he said. "I got Murray at my place, by the way, in case you were wondering."

"Murray?" I said. The name sounded familiar. "Murray who?"

He smiled and shook his head. "Claire's cat."

That was my wife's name—Claire. And hearing him say it made me feel cold inside all of a sudden.

"More power to you," I said.

He straightened up out of the engine and wiped his hands on a rag. "Look, Gary," he said. "I don't know quite how to bring this up, but I'm awful sorry. About what happened between me and Claire, I mean. I was drunk. I know that's no excuse but there it is. And you know yourself that Claire's always been a complicated woman." He kept wiping his hands with the rag, studying his fingernails. "But I swear to God we only did it that one time. I wanted you to know that. And we really didn't even actually do it exactly." He looked at me, blushed, folded the rag and stuck it in his pocket. "I mean we didn't have actual intercourse exactly."

My head pounded. I'd been nodding along like all this was no big deal. I wasn't sure what he wanted from me. "Well what exactly *did* you guys have?" I said.

Tom blushed some more. "Nothing," he said. "It was nothing. It was the stupidest thing I've ever done. I'm sorry for my part in this."

Then he told me to get in the truck and try her. I did. The engine cranked, almost caught, then died.

Tom leaned in with his screwdriver. "Try her again."

I kept thinking about what exactly Tom had done with my wife if it wasn't actual intercourse. I couldn't help wondering if it was something I'd never done with her. I kept hearing him say her name—Claire, Claire—as if that one word had a magic in it I'd never learned. To tell you the truth, him saying her name pissed me off worse than him fucking her—or whatever it was they did. I turned the ignition again and it started to catch. The truck was in first gear. My foot was on the clutch. I heard Tom say "Claire" again in the back of my head and I popped the clutch. The truck lurched forward with a thud, then stalled, and Tom fell to the side clutching his groin. I jumped out.

"Jesus, Tom, I'm sorry," I said and I really was. "Are you okay?"

Tom was groaning low in his throat, trying to catch his breath. When I helped him to his feet, I saw the piss stain start in his crotch and work its way down his leg. I'd never seen a grown man piss himself sober. He stood stooped over, eyes closed.

"Did I get you in the balls?" I said and I couldn't help but giggle a little. But then he crumpled to the ground again. His eyes glazed over and he gasped for air.

"Call 911," he said.

Oh Jesus, I thought. Why does every goddamn thing have to happen to me?

Goddamn Me

But just in case you thought things would end up all hopeless and helpless and depressing—well, goddamn me if you ain't got another think coming.

Old Tom ruptured his bladder and spent four days in the hospital but he bounced right back and didn't even sue me for anything past the medical bills which my homeowner's liability covered minus the deductible. And after that we got to be pretty close. He stopped over one night about a week after his discharge and we both apologized like crazy—me for slamming him with the truck (I told him my foot slipped off the clutch which the more I think about it I'm beginning to believe is the truth) and him for not exactly having actual intercourse with Claire (which I don't even care what they did anymore, be it heavy petting or swapping underwear, but you can't blame a guy for being curious). We talked for a while about this and that, and when I finally asked him if he minded if I got myself a drink, Tom said not at all.

"Mind getting me one too?" he said.

Turns out he'd had a lot of time to think in the hospital and he'd decided he wasn't an alcoholic. Not really. Most of that A.A. business just didn't apply to him, he said. He was just a guy who enjoyed his drinks. Enjoyed them too much sometimes, sure, but that didn't mean he had to totally give up drinking. He just had to watch himself.

"Nothing wrong with a few drinks as long as you don't go on a bender. Now the guys at A.A. would say I'm in denial, but they don't know me like you do." He took a sip of his bourbon and smiled slow. "Do you think I'm an alcoholic?" he said.

"Not for me to say," I told him.

"Come on. You can tell me the truth."

I laughed. "No goddamn way, Tom," I said. "No more than I am."

Tom smiled. "Guys like us who like our drinks, we have to look out for each other. First rule is never drink alone. That's the biggest sign you have a problem. Second rule, no drinking till after work. Third rule, when your buddy says you've had enough, you've had enough."

And so far everything's been working out fine for the both of us. Tom got me a job working for him in maintenance and he's the best boss I ever had. I'm learning how to fix something different every day. Meantime we got my truck up and running better than ever. He helped me install a new garbage disposal and we rewired my circuit box. Next week we're putting in a new AC compressor he got for cost and believe it or not I'm thinking about shingling the goddamn roof.

Every goddamn thing just couldn't be better.

And just last night we were sitting on Tom's front porch having a couple of drinks. Murray the cat was sitting on Tom's lap purring away and I actually reached over and scratched the goddamn thing behind the ears if you can believe that. Tom poured me another glass of Jim Beam and said, "That's your last one tonight, pal."

"Damn right, partner," I said.

Then Tom said, "You know, it makes no sense both of us living alone right next to each other. Waste of money. Let's face it, Gary, your wife's never coming back."

I lifted my glass. "Praise God."

"You oughta put your house on the market and move in with me. You'll get the equity from your house and I could use the rent."

And the more I thought about it the better the idea sounded. It sounded so good we ruled ourselves another drink and clinked glasses to seal the deal. By the time I got up to go home, I felt like howling at the moon. Everything was perfect now that Claire was out of the picture. Murray zigzagged back and forth in front of me chasing shadows and I followed him step for step.

THE GARDEN

I'd only had one drink on the day of the accident. Eva was working till midnight at the hospital, which meant the boys'd be waiting for me to make dinner. But I didn't feel like going home just yet. A.B. and Reed could wait. They knew the rules: no friends in the house, no TV until homework was finished, no fighting.

That last one was the rule they broke all the time, but they seemed to fight more when I was around than when I wasn't, at least to hear Eva tell it. "They're competing for your attention," she claimed.

"I give them my attention," I told her. "How much attention they want?"

"All of it," she said. "You have to teach them to share."

"Hell, Eva, I work all day. How about you teaching them?"

"I work too," she said.

This was true, but only lately. Eva'd finished up her Associate's in Radiography at Florida State College in Jacksonville that previous spring and got the first job she'd had since we were married, shooting x-rays at Flagler Hospital about a half-hour away. Took her five years of night classes to get a two-year degree. I sometimes thought I earned that degree as much as she did, what with all the time I spent babysitting the boys while she was off bettering herself. Course, it was all worth it. Now that she was bringing home a paycheck, we could save up to move out of that cramped two-bedroom out in the sticks. The boys sharing bunk beds sure didn't help keep peace in the household.

"You're their father," Eva said. "It's your job to teach them."

So I tried. I tried to teach them. They were brothers. I expected them to act like brothers. Stand up for each other. I tried to be patient, something I never got from *my* old man. The results? A.B., 12, voice changing but still cracking high when he got excited, went on about how he'd act like a brother soon as Reed quit bossing him around. "Talk to *him*," he'd say. "*He* started it." Reed, 13 and hitting his growth, played it cool. "Yes, sir," he'd say. "I'll do better next time, sir." Which set A.B. off even worse. "Liar," he'd say. "Don't believe him, Dad. He's *always* sucking up to you." Meantime Reed calmly inspected his hands, cracked his knuckles one by one until A.B. screamed at him to stop it. "See?" A.B. would explode, damn near tears by now. "He *always* starts it!"

I'd built myself a big shed out in the back yard, right next to my vegetable garden, and sometimes I spent whole evenings out there, from end of dinner till bedtime, just so I wouldn't have to listen to them. The shed was wired for electric so I could use it as a workshop, and I'd open the padlock, turn on the window unit AC, and find a ballgame or a country station on the radio. I'd spend hours tinkering with a broken appliance or cleaning my guns. I kept a bottle out there, too. Anything for a little peace.

So when my foreman Butch Hodakowitz invited me for drinks after work that day, I figured what the hell. One drink. I didn't make a habit of drinking at a bar when I could drink cheaper at home, but it was payday, Butch said the first round was on him, and it'd been one hell of a day at the paper mill.

I polished my first drink off pronto, pushed back from the table.

"You ain't leaving already," Butch said.

"Boys're home alone."

"Ain't they old enough to take care of themselves by now?"

"Eva doesn't like them on their own too much."

"Hell, when my kids were that age, me and the wife would leave 'em for two weeks while we took vacation. Relax, Lamb. You'll spoil those boys rotten. Have another drink."

"You didn't take your kids on vacation with you?" I asked.

Butch looked at me like I'd just pissed in his beer. "Now what would be the point of that?" he said. "Whose vacation would that be?"

I stood up.

"Aw, hell, don't go, Lamb," Butch said. "I took 'em plenty of places. Speaking of, full moon this weekend, Lamb. Taking the dogs out. Bring your boys along. Bet they never went coon hunting."

"Thanks," I said. "They're booked up with ballgames this weekend."

"Maybe just me and you, then."

"I'll check and see what Eva's got planned for me."

I stepped outside, hopped in my truck and headed south, figuring I'd stop at the ABC on my way home. I felt bad about lying to Butch, but I was too embarrassed to tell him the truth. The boys didn't have any ballgames, and there was no way I was taking A.B. shooting again, not for a while anyway, not after last week.

•

It happened on my and A.B.'s birthday, a Saturday this year. Actually, mine fell three days later, but I'd taken to celebrating it on the same day as his. Easier that way. So that morning, Eva made a big batch of birthday pancakes, candles and all, and I brought in A.B.'s present from the shed where I'd been hiding it.

"Where's your brother?" I asked Reed.

He shrugged. "Not my turn to watch him."

"Reed."

"Still in bed."

"Roust him," I said. "We got plans."

Course, soon as A.B. came out still rubbing sleep from his eyes and saw that long skinny package, there went the surprise. He'd been waiting for it ever since he didn't get it for Christmas and spent a solid week moping and complaining, and now he tore into the wrapping, scattering it like a hound digging up a gopher hole.

I'd bought him his first rifle, a Winchester "Yellow Boy" that cost me a pretty penny, I don't mind telling you. Eva hadn't exactly been in favor, but Reed had gotten his first rifle when he was 12, and I couldn't very well pass on A.B., even if he wasn't as mature and serious as his brother at that age. Besides, they'd both had air rifles since third grade, and I'd taught them how to respect a firearm.

And when he held that rifle in his hands, the look on his face made it all worthwhile.

"Wow!" he said. "This one's even better'n Reed's!"

A.B. was all fired up to hit the woods now, but Reed said, "What about Dad's presents?" so I went ahead and opened mine. Eva got me a polo shirt and pair of khakis I knew I'd only wear when she told me to, and Reed gave me one of those Weed Weasels you see advertised on TV. "This'll make my gardening a breeze," I said. "I was just fixing to turn the soil over for a second planting."

"That's nothing," A.B. said, jostling past his brother and laying a gift bag in my lap.

Reed gritted his teeth. A.B. hung over my shoulder while I peeked inside the bag. "Open it, Dad!" he said, practically jumping up and down with excitement. "Come *on!*"

Nestled in crumpled purple tissue paper was a stainless steel hip flask in a leather sheath. The flask was full, too. I opened it, sniffed, put it to my lips.

"Honey," Eva said, laughing. "It's seven in the morning!"

"It's Jameson's Irish," A.B. said proudly. "The rest of the bottle's in your liquor cabinet. It cost plenty, but I told the guy I wanted something special for a special dad."

"I was mortified," Eva said. "He wouldn't let me just buy it, no, he had to tell the clerk he was buying it, and then he had to ask a million questions. I thought I'd get arrested for contributing to the delinquency! 'Allen Bennet Lamb,' I said. 'Liquor is no kind of present for a boy to give his father!' But he wouldn't take no for an answer."

I held up the flask, balanced it in the palm of my hand. "It's perfect," I said. I stood then, ruffled A.B.'s hair, slipped the flask in my hip pocket.

"What should I do with this?" Reed said, holding up the Weed Weasel box. He'd already picked up the wrappings and threw them in the trash.

"Just put it on my workbench," I said, handing him my key to the shed. "I'll get to it later. Grab your rifle while you're out there. We're going shooting." I rubbed my hands together. "Time for the birthday boy to break in his present."

I didn't bring my rifle. I liked hunting but wasn't much for target shooting, and that's all I'd planned for them today. I took them to a stretch of woods west of St. Augustine. We hiked through scrub pine down a narrow path flanked by palmetto and Spanish bayonet. Up ahead was a clearing I knew where they could shoot. Reed took the point, and I took the rear. A.B. marched between us, head jerking this way and that every time he heard the slightest noise. He'd always been a jumpy kid, the exact opposite of his brother. You could set a bomb off next to Reed and he wouldn't even flinch.

I heard something rustle in the brush ahead, and Reed stopped, rifle held ready.

"What is it?" A.B. shouted, running to catch up. He stumbled, lurched forward, his rifle stock slamming Reed between the shoulder blades.

Reed staggered but quickly caught his balance. "Just a corn snake," he said, and I saw it unravel itself quick as a flash across the path and into the brush on the other side.

"Good thing your mother's not here," I joked. She had a thing about snakes.

Then A.B. elbowed past his brother, raising his rifle and aiming into the thicket, but Reed stopped him, his hand steering the muzzle skyward.

"Watch out where you're pointing that," he said.

A.B. wrenched the rifle away. "*You* watch out!"

"Enough!" I said, coming up behind them. I put my hand on A.B.'s trembling shoulder. He had a fuse shorter than his attention span. "Point that rifle down and away," I said. "You got to keep your head, son." I squeezed his shoulder. "Is the safety on?"

"Yeah," A.B. said. He stared hard at Reed, who turned away with a shrug.

"You sure?" I said. "Check it for me."

He fumbled with the switch. "It's on," he said.

"Keep it shouldered till we hit the clearing, son. Too tight for shooting here."

"Tell Reed that," A.B. said.

"I'm telling you both. Wait'll we get to the clearing."

Reed gave me a dark look as if to say, "You ain't telling me shit." And he was right. I didn't have to tell Reed anything.

It was barely eight o'clock, and my shirt was already soaked through. The air was dead and heavy. I slowed my pace, let the boys put some distance between me and them, but not so far that I couldn't keep an eye out. I slipped the flask out of my hip pocket, took a long swallow. The heat hit my stomach, and then I took another swallow, felt the gooseflesh raise my hackles.

There's a moment of clarity that comes with your first drink of the day. It doesn't last long, and when it's over, it's over, no matter how hard you chase after it. While the moment lasts, though, it brings a crystal focus to the world that's hard to improve on.

I took another swallow and watched my sons walking down the path before me. Reed stepped ahead, nimble as a deer, rifle low, close-cropped head turning easy from side to side, dark eyes taking in every detail. I saw a lot of myself in that boy. He'd do well, better than me, I hoped, as long as he went to college. I'd never have to worry about him.

A.B., on the other hand, him I worried about. A.B. daydreamed along ten paces behind his brother, kicking at the underbrush, his rifle slung idly over his shoulder, the barrel bouncing against his neck with every step. He looked to the left, to the right, to the left again, down at his feet, his eyes in constant motion, covering every angle but taking in nothing. He looked to the sky, grinned wide at the sun, and then tripped over something, looked down to see what it was. He turned around, caught me staring at him, and laughed.

"Have a nice trip?" he called, and he faked tripping again. "See you next fall!"

I shook my head, laughing despite myself, and I thought of how different my two sons were, and how a father's love is supposed to be unconditional and equal, and I knew this could never be. One son will find favor, while the other turns his face away, his teeth on edge with envy. I knew this to be a sad truth, and I also knew there was nothing I could do about it. This had been the way of the world since time began.

When we reached the clearing, I sent the boys in search of targets, not too hard to find since somebody'd been using the place as a dump. We set up bottles and cans, and the boys fired away. Reed patiently picked off every can and bottle he set his sights on, but A.B. was having a hard time coming within five feet of the barn's broad side. He complained about the rifle's kick, claimed the barrel must be bent, blamed the sun in his eyes, the heat of the day, the loud reports from Reed's marksmanship.

"Stupid gun!" he said, finally.

Reed approached him. "Try holding it like this."

"Don't touch it!" A.B. shouted. "It's mine."

"Okay, okay," Reed said. "How about a bigger target?" He ran off to find one.

"Keep your eyes open and squeeze nice and easy," I said. "Just like I taught you."

"I am," he pouted.

"No you're not," I said. "You're yanking on the trigger."

"I am not!"

"Then do it your way," I said, suddenly losing all patience. "I don't give a good goddamn if you hit anything or not."

"Here!" I heard Reed call from the edge of the clearing, and I caught him out of the corner of my eye holding up an old five-gallon paint bucket. He laughed. "Even you couldn't miss this!"

I turned my back and walked off, reaching automatically for the flask in my pocket. But it was empty by this time. Damn thing only held a pint.

Then I heard the shot and Reed's hissing curse. I whirled around in time to see the paint bucket go skittering across the ground, Reed staring wide-eyed at his now empty hand. He put it to his mouth.

A.B. lowered his rifle. "Da-ad," he sang. "Reed said the fuck word."

And that's when I hit him. I didn't know what else to do.

I never told Eva what happened that day, and neither did the boys. I only told her she was right. A.B. was too young for a rifle. He was on full restriction, I said, and Eva didn't question me. A.B. spent the rest of that day in his room, and I spent the day in the shed. I had a drink. I had another. I finished off the Jameson's, started in on a bottle of vodka. I cleaned and oiled the Winchester, put it up in the rafters out of reach. Then I took the Weed Weasel out of its box, laid out the parts on my workbench, and immediately lost interest. I poured myself another. I sat down in my easy chair and took a swallow.

It was dusk when I woke up. I opened the shed door and saw Reed out there tilling my garden. The assembled Weed Weasel leaned against the shed, crusted with dirt, while Reed put his back into his spadework, furrowing the topsoil in neat, straight lines.

"What's wrong with the Weasel?" I said.

"Piece of crap." He stopped, leaned on his shovel, wiped sweat from his face. A band-aid ringed his left index finger where the bucket handle had broken skin.

"You okay?" I said. "I guess I should've asked you already."

"I'm okay." He made a fist, testing it. "Don't know about A.B., though." He opened his mouth, closed it. He kicked at a clod of dirt with the toe of his boot. His voice was low, uneasy. "When are you going to do something about him?"

"Like what?"

"Like help him."

"Help him how?"

"I don't know," he said. "Can't you talk to him?"

"I've talked myself blue."

"Then take him to a shrink," Reed said. "He's crazy, you know."

"Don't say that."

"You should hear him. You don't know what he's like."

I'd already turned my back. I raised my head to the sky. The sun was setting behind a thick purple scatter of clouds. I tend to take our sunsets for granted.

"Is your brother using drugs?" I said. "Is that what you're saying?"

Reed shook his head. "I wish," he said.

•

On my way home from drinks with Butch, I stopped at ABC Liquor for a bottle of Captain Morgan's Spiced Rum, my drink of choice for the past couple of weeks. I had a bottle at home, I knew, but not enough to get me through the night.

Tyler Herp was manning the register when I brought my

bottle up. "Morgan's goes on sale tomorrow," he said.

"Good," I told him. "I'll be back for more."

I drove home, pulled in the carport, and let myself into the kitchen. "Yo, ho, ho," I called. "Dad's home."

I could hear the TV going in the boys' room, but otherwise it was quiet. I didn't bother calling again. I didn't feel like dealing with anybody till I'd had a drink.

Eva'd left a note on the counter below the liquor cabinet. There was a tuna-noodle casserole in the fridge, it said, and it let me know how long and at what temperature to cook it, as if I hadn't been cooking the lion's share of meals around here the whole time she was in school. I poured the last of last night's bottle of Captain Morgan's over ice in my big glass, and I splashed some Coke over the top, stirred it with my finger. I licked that finger and took a nice, long drink. I threw the empty bottle in the trash and stashed the new bottle back in the cabinet.

I turned on the oven and put the casserole in. I sat at the kitchen table, sipping my drink and staring out the window. Then I noticed the garden out back.

Me and Reed had planted rows of beans, peppers, and tomatoes right after my birthday, and now somebody had tore through them, uprooting every damn plant and chopping them into a muddy mess of salad and stalk. That damn Weed Weasel was planted handle first in the center of the garden, mean wheels full of sharp teeth glinting in the westering sun. The shed door hung half open, padlock ripped from the frame.

"Sweet Jesus," I whispered. "A.B., Goddamn you straight to hell."

I was plenty mad, you bet, but I just sat there a minute, too stunned to move. My legs felt weak, my arms barely strong enough to hold my head in my hands. I finished my drink, rattled the ice cubes in the bottom of my glass. I thought about making another. I could make myself another now, or I could wait until after I settled this matter with A.B. I had no idea what I was going to say to him. I couldn't imagine.

•

This last part's tough to tell, tough to keep clear. Let's face it: I was drunk. It doesn't take a rocket scientist to figure I was an alcoholic. Still am, according to the 12-steppers, and they may be wrong about a lot else, but that's one thing they got right.

When I walked into the boys' bedroom, Reed was lying on the bottom bunk, eyes closed, TV tuned to a 24-hour local news station. "Another senseless tragedy on the city's south side," the announcer was saying when I turned it off. Reed opened his eyes. He blanched at the sight of me. His face was streaked with tears, his clothes and hands caked with dirt. He had a long cut over his left eye.

"What happened?" I said. "Where's your brother?"

Reed rolled out of bed and stood up, his fists clenching and unclenching. He glanced at the unmade upper bunk, as if he expected to see A.B. there, and then his dark eyes fell. He struggled to catch his breath.

"Did he do that to my garden?" I said.

"No, sir," Reed answered, voice tight and trembling. "Not all of it. Just the first part. After that…"

He choked, his voice gave out on him, and then he started sobbing so bad I could barely understand him. He said he was sorry. He said it was all his fault. He said he didn't mean to do it. He said he wished he were dead. He turned and punched the metal frame of the upper bunk as hard as he could again and again. I grabbed ahold of him, turned him to face me, got him in a bear hug to try to calm him down.

"God," he breathed, his eyes wild, nostrils flaring. "You stink of booze!"

"Where is your brother?"

When I opened the door to the shed, I saw it was way too late to do anything. The Winchester lay on the floor beside him. I bent down and rolled him over. The bullet had made a small hole in his forehead before taking the back of his skull off. His eyes were open and so glassy I could practically see my reflection in them. I closed them, smoothed the bangs off his forehead, and called 911. There wasn't anything else to do for him.

I called Eva at the hospital so she'd hear it from me first, and then I went back to see about Reed. He was sitting on the floor of his bedroom, rocking and moaning low in his throat, but he took one look at me, my hands covered with his brother's blood, and went berserk. He tore at his hair, beat his head on the floor, shrieking like a soul burning in torment. "Hush," I cried, hugging him tight, squeezing the very breath out of him. "It was an accident," I said, over and over. "An accident."

·

The court took it easy on poor Reed, remanding him to the state mental facility for treatment. He's come a long way there, considering, and our weekly visits have gotten more bearable, though poor Eva still cries half the way home. She says he doesn't have a kid's eyes any more. I can't help but agree, but then again, I'm not sure he ever did. Reed never much acted like a kid. I guess I never let him know it was expected of him.

So life goes on. We sold the house that first year and moved here to Ocala. I got an okay job, and Eva's working for a family practice. She sees a therapist once a week, and she recently stopped taking the Zoloft. Me, I'm still toughing it out alone.

But last night, I damn near broke into that bottle of Captain Morgan's, the same one I bought the evening of the accident, the one I left unopened in the liquor cabinet, the one I carefully packed and unpacked when we moved here. That unopened bottle's been my unspoken penance, something Eva can't understand, just like I can't understand how she can still burst into tears after more than three years, like she did last night lying next to me in bed. I tried to soothe her, as usual, rubbing her back and telling her hush, honey, it's all over, there's nothing we can do, but she suddenly turned to me, eyes burning.

Darling, I thought, please don't start.

"I can't keep it inside any longer," she said. "Sometimes, I can't help it, I'm glad it was A.B. instead of Reed. If it was Reed who died, I don't think I could stand it." Her voice shivered, a kind of giggled sob. "Isn't that awful?" she said.

I closed my eyes, tried to picture Reed on the floor of the shed, but I couldn't. It was A.B. It was always A.B. He would always be the one.

CALL

The phone rings. We answer. "Hello?" we say, and we say this hopefully, hoping beyond hope that this is the call we've been waiting for all our lives. "Oh," we say. "No. We are not at all interested in your product. Frankly, we are disappointed in the nature of your call." We hang up.

We take our dinner out of the freezer. We are not at all interested in our dinner, but we must eat it nonetheless.

The phone rings. We answer. "Fine, thank you," we say, "and you?" We listen. We put our dinner in the microwave, set the timer, place dish, cutlery, and paper napkin on our galley kitchen counter. "No," we say. "We rent an efficiency apartment and, as such, haven't the authority to authorize the sort of installation you wish to install."

The microwave beeps. We are not at all interested in our dinner, and yet we spoon it onto our dish, stand at our galley kitchen counter and fork food into our mouth. We are not especially pleased with our dinner, but we are presently watching our weight—at present, we meant to say—and we understand that weight watching requires the regular intake of calorically-monitored meals, especially pleasing or not. We chew. We swallow.

The phone rings.

We eye the phone warily. We are beginning to perceive a pattern here. We have perceived patterns in the past, and we have adjusted our behavior accordingly to fit the parameters of each pattern we've seen. We could let our answering machine answer, but we've grown to distrust our normally sober voice's cheery simulacrum, which rarely persuades callers to leave messages. We wouldn't want to miss our call if this is in fact the call we've been waiting for all our lives. We understand there is that chance, however slim. We have perceived patterns, but we find ourselves splashing through the shallow puddle of hope that wells in our heart. We answer.

"Hello?" we say, and we say this hopefully, hoping beyond hope that this is indeed our call, the call we've been waiting for, the call that will change our lives in indescribably delicious ways.

We are bound to be disappointed.

•

We fear parties, but our project manager has invited us by e-mail memo, and so we must go. We especially fear living rooms at parties, the established groups of smugly winking colleagues, each in his or her proper section. We avoid the cross-hierarchical banter, the carefully-circulated innuendo, the cycled and recycled brainstorms and discoveries, the strategic drainage of bracing cocktails. Ice cubes ring. Voices rise and fall. A new hire unaccountably barks with laughter, and her fellows step back, reconfigure alliances. We edge our way past the dining room buffet. Our colleagues glance up from plates piled with hummus and pita wedges, dilled broccoli florets and flayed shrimp. "Oh," they say, looking at a spot on the wall just behind us. "Hi, there."

"Eat up!" our project manager cries, slapping backs and squeezing shoulders. He glances our way, slips his free hand into his pocket. He sips from the glass in his other hand. "Have something, why don't you," he says. We select an olive from a platter, arrange a spot in our cheek for it, and smile, mandible cringing sourly all the way to our ear. Our project manager opens his mouth, closes it. "Plenty more," he says, turning away. "Plenty for everyone."

We know something of this world. We know there is never plenty for everyone.

We visit the bathroom, where, business finished, we make a secret show of running water in the sink, moistening fingertips, drying them daintily on the apparently unused guest towel. We don't make a habit of lathering our hands at other people's homes. We don't care to get started. We consider ourselves in the mirror, wishing we could grow accustomed to our reflection, but we never seem to. We always appear somewhat surprised in mirrors.

There is a knock at the door. "Somebody die in there or what?" a nasal alto sings.

We open the door. A young woman squeezes past us, heels tapping a pigeon-toed flamenco on ceramic tile. "Hold this," she giggles, handing us a long-stemmed glass of wine. "Not to be rude, but I'm doing the tinkle dance here." She rushes to the toilet, already hiking hem of black shift to hips of white pantyhose. "Close the door?" she says. "I won't be long."

We stand in the hallway, wine in hand. We sniff it: Pouilly-Fuissé. Our doctors have advised against alcohol.

The toilet flushes, the faucet runs at length, the door opens. The young woman sighs, smoothes her boxy dress across her hips. We do not know her. New hire, perhaps, or unmet spouse of unknown colleague. She smiles at us in a way that reminds us of one of our own ex-spouses. The same tauntingly innocent eyes scrutinizing us with judicious glee. The same large-boned figure burdened by blunt sexuality. She is young enough to be the eldest daughter of that particular ex-spouse, though our brief union bore no fruit.

None of our unions has ever proven fruitful.

"Thanks," she says, taking her glass, fingers brushing ours on its stem. "You work here?"

"Here?" we say.

"Not here. With these people, I mean."

"Yes," we say, "though we work alone."

"A loner," she says, eyes glittering. "What do you do?"

"We crunch entities."

"Royal we or plural?"

"Generic."

"Catchy," she says, tugging at the bunched bodice of her polyester frock. "You're staring at my dress. You find it incredibly ugly."

"W—"

"It's my father's fault. When I was a girl, he bought me incredibly ugly clothes to keep the boys away. Didn't work. Only made me want to get naked at every opportunity. As you can see, though, I never developed a sense of fashion. Are you on Prozac by any chance?"

"No," we say.

"Have you considered it?"

"We have considered and tried all types of pharmaceuticals, but we've found the ballyhooed benefits to be contraindicated by the concomitant ennui."

"I hear you," she says. "You should try BuSpar. Prozac kept me up all night. Zoloft made me wish I were depressed again. I won't even *mention* the Xanax problem. But I'm happy with the BuSpar. *Way* happy. They should put it in the drinking water, like fluoride." She winks, thumbs us in the ribs, titters fetchingly. "What sort of entities did you say you crunch?"

"The generally more abstract or abstruse ones."

"E.g.?"

"Phonemes, morphemes, allomorphs, et al."

"I.e.?"

"Ciphers, gnoses, n-dimensional deconstruction of zero-element values."

"The devil's in the details, I'm guessing." She leans forward, rests elbows on our shoulders, wine glass suspended by dainty fingers in our peripheral vision, her face close to ours. "Are you here alone?"

"We are generally everywhere alone."

"Lucky for me," she says, trailing turquoise nails over the skin of our scalp. "I crave mystery. It turns me on. Care to come to my place? You don't know me. I don't work here. I'm the neighbor. There's always a neighbor at these kinds of parties."

"We'd only disappoint you, as we have countless others."

"Best come-on line I've heard all night. Wait." She touches a finger to our lips. "Don't say no. Think about it. If not now, some other time." She selects a felt-tip from our pocket protector, scribbles a number on the palm of our hand. "Call me," she says.

We stare at our hand, each digit displaying its own unique value. "We need to use the facilities again," we say.

"I like that in a man," the neighbor murmurs, and, giving our hand a parting, promissory squeeze, she returns down the hallway to the party.

We go back into the bathroom, close and lock the door, run scalding water in the sink, and, despite ourselves, work up a formidable lather. The neighbor's number washes clean. We lather again. Our reflection stares at us.

The appearance of surprise is the only thing that seems to surprise us anymore.

•

Our computer monitor chimes. We save and send our work, save and send it again. We've learned not to trust the prevailing technology. We pack our briefcase and exit our cubicle. It is after hours. We generally try to arrive and depart before and after hours. We negotiate a maze of phosphorescent cubicles, corridors mapped by limbic memory.

"Whoah!" our project manager gasps, rounding a corner. "You spooked me!" He steps back, brushes his shirtfront. "Working late again?"

"Yes."

"Don't overdo it," he says. "Mustn't neglect your family. After all, what's more important?"

"We have no family."

"Oh. Well. Good. That you're not neglecting anyone. Um. Generic, isn't it? I remember asking already."

"We really must be going."

"Good. My point exactly. Good job on that last project, by the way. Good work all around. How's the current project?"

"Finished."

"Good. Well. Um. New project coming up next week, you probably got the memo."

"Yes."

"This one scares me a little, I don't mind telling you. Ontological Warranty Division ordered it, so it's your standard redundant tautologics, but it's not as pointless as I'd like it to be. It's actually for a guidance system." He shudders. "I hate guidance systems. I'm comfortable managing a completely pointless project purely for love of the process, but as soon as your project involves a destination, well, then it's got a point, doesn't it. And if your project has a point, even a teensy one, your results are under scrutiny. You miss the point, all of a sudden they're talking about restructuring your career objectives. That's what happened to the last job on my resume. I missed the point. Whole de*part*ment missed the point. Never even knew there was a point." He chuckles ruefully. "Not to say we have anything to worry about here, of course. There's always another project, ninety-nine-point-nine percent of them completely pointless. Still. I worry. I have to worry. Comes with the position. Power worries. Not for you to worry. Not your job. I'll do all the worrying."

"We're not worried."

"You look like a worrier, is why I mentioned it in the first place. Probably because of the hair thing. I know you told me awhile ago." He scratches his head. "Chemo, is it?"

"Male pattern gone amuck."

"You don't say. Eyebrows too?"

"Perfectly harmless if rather anomalous reaction to stress, the doctors say."

"Then *you* are a worrier."

"We used to worry about going bald," we say. "Not anymore."

"I worry about everything," our project manager says. "That's my job. I heard the other day that somebody discovered neutrinos have mass. One day they don't, next day they do. Go figure. Infinitesimally eensy-weensy-beensy mass, but mass is mass. This is the kind of news that keeps me up at night. What next?" He raises a hand as if to touch us but apparently reconsiders. "By the way," he says, "who was that cute number I saw you with at the party?"

"Your neighbor," we say.

"Really?" He tugs meditatively at his ear lobe. "Can't place her." He laughs, turns to walk away. "If I didn't know better, I'd say my memory's shot."

•

The phone rings. The microwave beeps. We are beginning to perceive a pattern.

"Hello?" we say, and we say this as hopefully as we are able. "No," we say, "we are not at all interested. We were just preparing to eat our dinner. Our dinner does not especially please us, but we must eat it nonetheless. No," we say, "there is perhaps no better time to call. The past is impossible, the future unproven, and the present gone even as we speak."

The phone beeps.

"Excuse us for a moment momentarily." We press flash.

"It's me," our project manager's neighbor breathes. "Do you even know my name?"

"No."

"I don't know yours either. Your boss gave me your number, but he couldn't remember your name."

"We have a caller waiting on Call Waiting."

"Call me back. Do you still have my number?"

"No."

"Men," she sighs, and she gives us her number again. "Call me right back. Promise."

We promise. We press flash again. "Please don't ever call us again," we say, and we hang up. We call our project manager's neighbor back.

"Psychic Hotline," she answers. "Now I know your name. Caller I.D. I'd be lost without it. So," she drawls coyly, "is this your real name or a fake phonebook name?"

"Real."

"How marvelously ordinary. The perfect alias, a name that couldn't attract attention if it tried. You know," she whispers, "I can't stop thinking of you. I know where you live. Why don't I come over?"

"We don't take visitors."

"Then you come here."

"We're waiting for a call."

"Let your machine take it."

"It's not that kind of call."

"What kind is it?"

"We're not certain. We've been expecting this call all our lives it seems to us, but the exact nature of the call still eludes us, as does the call itself."

"Could you be more, you know...specific?"

We hesitate. "All right," we say, finally. "It happened late one night so long ago that it almost feels as though it happened to some other person. We were sleeping, dreaming a dream whose outcome we were convinced was somehow crucial to our well-being, when suddenly the phone rang. We reached for the bedside phone, groggily said, 'Hello?' and waited. There was no response, but in that brief interval of waiting, we felt a great yawning maw of power opening up through the phone line. We felt a sudden rush of pure joy such as we had never experienced before, and we waited breathlessly for whoever or whatever was on the other end to speak. We felt clearly that whatever message we were about to hear would change our lives in indescribably delicious ways we can't begin to imagine."

"What happened then?"

We grimace, embarrassed. "In our excitement, we accidentally fumbled and dropped the receiver, disconnecting ourselves."

"And you've been waiting for a call-back ever since?"

"What other reason is there for picking up the phone?"

"Communication, for one."

"Ninety-nine-point-nine percent unnecessary."

"It's what we're doing now."

"In a manner of speaking."

"What does your therapist say about this? I'm assuming you're seeing one."

"Several," we say. "And they all say about what you'd expect."

"Vultures," she says scornfully. "I'm touching myself, you know."

"Excuse us?"

"I'm touching myself while you talk to me. I'm lying naked on my bed, touching myself, you know, down there. It's the latest thing. Vox pop copulatus. There's a thriving Ma and Pa telecommunications industry devoted to it."

"So we've been led to believe. Books making excessive use of quotation marks are documenting the phenomenon. Pulses are rising over board-room speaker phones."

"Your voice excites me," she says. "There's a certain timbre to it that moistens my innermost recesses of desire. Wow. Saying that excites me even more. Does it excite you? Would you like to touch yourself, too?"

"We don't touch ourselves anymore," we say, "except in an unavoidably incidental or clinical manner."

"Good. I don't like men who touch themselves while I talk to them. I like men to pay attention to what I'm saying, not yank their pesky crankies. Do you like women who touch themselves while you talk to them?"

"We have no strong feelings on the subject."

"Not good enough," she says, voice husky. "Tell me."

In times past, we acquiesce to tell her, we have enjoyed several women who touched themselves while we talked to them and/or while they talked to us. One of our ex-spouses liked to touch herself while she spoke to us in Spanish. We never learned Spanish. We know a little French, enough to get by, but not enough to touch oneself to. Another of our ex-spouses enjoyed touching herself whether we talked to her or not. We were forever entering one room or another of the house to discover her splayed dumbstruck on whatever surface had apparently presented itself as most convenient when the urge struck, busily touching herself, unaware of our very presence. "But we never held it against her," we hasten to add. "The divorce had more to do with her spending than her touching."

"*Oh!*" she says. "Nnnnnnnn!"

"Excuse us?"

"I just came." She sighs dreamily. "The key to good sex is forgetting who you think you are for one brief warbling moment." Her voice catches. "But how can something so completely transmogrifying make me feel so utterly myself when it's over?"

"That's been our experience as well."

"Did you come too?"

"Hardly. We don't do that anymore."

"Not at all?"

"Our penis rises, our penis sets. It's all the same to us."

"Oh why, *why*, why must I always fall for pale, limp weirdos?" Her lament ends with a brusque whimper. "Gotta run now. Afterplay's a letdown. Call me," she says. "I'll be waiting."

.

A freckled clerk at Telecom Outlet bags our purchase. "So I gotta ask," he says. "You got a mouse in your pocket?"

"Excuse us?"

"What's with the *we* biz? Who's *we*?"

"That would be 'Who *are* we?'"

"If you want to get grammatical." He sniffs, brushing a longish lock of carroty hair from his eyes. "No skin off my buns if you tell me or not."

"One of our therapists suggested that we need to relate more closely to humanity."

His eyes inexplicably moisten. "That's pitiful," he says, handing us our package.

Safely back in our efficiency, we phone our phone company, subscribe to its Caller I.D. service, plug in our new monitor.

The phone rings.

We check the monitor. We do not recognize the name or number. Our heart wells. Surely, the call we have been waiting for all our lives will not originate from familiar territory. "Hello?" we say, our voice trembling with possibility.

"I'm touching myself."

"Not now," we say. "We're busy."

"Doing what?"

"Waiting."

She tisks. "Your message has been garbled in transmission," she says. "I'm reading confusion amid great longing. You need me. Admit it."

"We're afraid you don't know us very well."

"What's to know?" she says. "You're a man with a past, preferably a tragic one. You built an empire and watched it crumble. You've loved and lost more times than you can remember, but still you can't stop hoping. Stop me if I'm getting warmer."

We make no response.

"It's true," she says. "I'm the answer to the question posed by your incredibly empty life. Blink once for yes, twice for no. Oh!" she moans. "Nnn*nnn*nn!"

We hang up.

The phone rings. We check our monitor, choose not to answer. Our answering machine picks up, our own voice unaccountably cheerful. "This is the Psychic Hotline," her message says. "Your problem is you can't stand yourselves. I'm the solution. Call before it's too late."

•

The phone rings. We check our monitor. We place our dinner in the microwave. The microwave beeps. The phone rings.

We call our project manager after hours, leave a message on his voice mail. "We will dot be id toborrow," we say. "We bust be comig dowd wid a code. We caddot crudge our eddidies. We deed our rest."

Days pass. Our dinner neither pleases nor displeases. We choose not to eat. We check our monitor. Some names and numbers originate from origins we recognize as having been somehow important once upon a time. Our laundry service calls us. Our therapists' offices call us. Our project manager calls us, tells us we're terminated in no uncertain terms. Our landlord calls us, notes we're dreadfully overdue. Our doctors' offices call us. Our power company calls us, tenders final notice.

We choose to answer only those calls which our monitor displays as a string of enigmatic hyphens. Phone solicitations, mostly, and we hang up as soon as they identify themselves as such. Still the phone rings. We check our monitor. We begin to forget what we're checking for. We begin to perceive a pattern. We have adjusted our behavior. We have been waiting all our lives. Our call will tell us something grand and true and fresh and nutritious and indubitably delicious about ourselves, something that will not only presently change our present at present but will retroactively change our past as well, will make our future as clean and sweet and new and improved as puddled honey 'neath a thriving hive of slap-sappy bee-bees.

Happy bees, we think we meant to say. We're no longer certain what we think we mean to say. "We feel biserable," we say. "We bust stay hobe again today."

The phone rings. From all across the planet, it seems, by day and night, we can hear the insistent music of its trilling tintinnabulation. We no longer recognize names or numbers. We stand at our galley kitchen counter, phone in hand.

"Hello?" we think we mean to say, and we think we mean to say this hopefully, fearfully, convinced that this is indeed our call. "Hello?"

A pair of hands snake up from behind us and cover our eyes. A warm body presses against our back. The phone drops from our limp grasp. "Guess who," she says.

We keep our eyes closed. "How did you get in?"

"I bribed the doorman."

"We have no doorman."

She backs away, and we hear the sound of a zipper unzipping, heavy fabric falling to the floor. "I climbed the fire escape and came in through a window."

"We have no windows."

"Neither healthy nor legal, I'd think." We hear the snap of elastic. "I came to help you."

"Impossible," we say.

"The possibilities are endless, but the truth is you left your door unlocked."

She grips our shoulder, turns us to face her. A pile of incredibly ugly clothing puddles at her feet. She leans forward, hands stroking, squeezing, face upturned, looming closer and closer, close enough for us to focus on our reflection in her widening pupils.

"Surprised?" she says, pushing us back against our galley kitchen counter.

She unbuttons our shirt, moves herself against us. We've lost all power. Her lips brush ours. A nervous digit traces a figure eight over and over in the cramped space between us.

"Come on," she purrs. "You knew it was me all along."

DIG

Since I can't seem to keep my mind on business this afternoon, I decide to leave the office early and surprise my wife. I stop at the 7-Eleven up the street and buy a single plastic-encased red rose.

"Have fun," the clerk says as she rings me up.

"Excuse me?"

She eyes me. "Never mind."

I slowly swing my Land Rover into our neighborhood. I happen to be the chairman of the Watch Committee for the Whispering Trace subdivision, a scrubbed and treeless peninsula of stucco ranch styles built on a sandy spit reclaimed from the former county landfill. My position requires that I keep my eyes peeled.

Across the cul-de-sac, the Lathams' yard man is blowing grass clippings off the driveway and into the street. I watch him a moment. He glances at me with hooded eyes, quickly looks away. Behind him, the front window blinds flutter.

I pull into our driveway. The door from the garage to the kitchen is unlocked.

I see my stepdaughters out the kitchen window, digging a hole in the back yard.

The screen door slams behind me.

"What have I told you about leaving the doors unlocked?"

Didi, eleven, dark, lean and sleek as an otter, stands at the rim of a three-foot wide, five-foot deep hole, clipboard in hand. She is my wife's daughter from her first marriage. She makes a careful notation on her legal pad and, without looking up, says, "He's home early."

Slaving away in the hole below is Leelee, ten, my wife's daughter from her second marriage. She wields her shovel with authority, fleshy back rippling with muscle beneath her sweat-stained t-shirt. She backhands a lock of muddy blonde hair from her eyes. "He's always home early," she says.

"Every day."

"Day after day."

Leelee heaves a clod of earth out of the hole. A rusty 9-volt battery pokes out of the scattered dirt. Didi nudges it with her sneakered toe, makes another notation. "And every day he's home earlier and earlier."

Leelee nods. "Pretty soon he'll leave work before he gets there."

"He'll be home all day."

"Every day."

"And then what will we do with him?"

"Where's your mother?" I say.

"Across the street," Leelee says.

"Visiting Mr. Latham."

"Mrs. Latham."

"That's right," Didi says. "Mrs. Latham."

I consider this for a moment. "Didn't I tell you," I say, "to quit digging holes in my back yard?"

"That was yesterday," Didi says.

"We quit digging yesterday," Leelee says.

"Are you saying quit digging yesterday and today?"

I hold the rose in my outstretched hands. "And tomorrow and tomorrow and tomorrow," I say.

Didi looks at the rose, sniffs. "Mom's right."

Leelee continues shoveling. "She usually is."

"About what?" I say.

"This," Didi says, sweeping an arm grandly, "is an archeological dig."

"It's our summer project," Leelee says.

"It's healthy educational exercise in the safety of our very own property."

I shake my head. "You're ruining my sod."

"Oh," Leelee murmurs tonelessly. "His sod."

Didi frowns. "Sod's much more important than archeological research."

"Why do something educational when we can watch TV instead?"

"Why watch TV when we can do drugs instead?"

"Why do drugs when we can—"

Leelee's shovel strikes something, a metallic ring interrupting her. She leans on her shovel, panting. "Oh… my… God," she breathes.

"What?" I say.

Didi drops her clipboard, eyes widening. "I can't believe it." She jumps in the hole. They huddle over something I can't see.

"Hey," I say, craning my neck. "What is it?"

The screen door slams, and I jump. The rose drops from my hand into the open pit.

"Well, well, well," my wife says breathlessly behind me. "Look who's finally home."

Her hand on my back seems almost weightless at first, but my fall into the pit remains endless.

TOUCHED

I saw the famous writer Ken Kesey address an auditorium of college students. Dressed in khaki shorts, desert boots, and pith helmet, he was on his way to Egypt, he said, to realize his lifelong dream of slipping a credit card between two stones of the Great Pyramid of Khufu. He held up the card for all to see. American Express, he said. The grand achievement of thousands of years of human evolution: thin, resilient, lightweight plastic—destined to outlast any old pyramid.

He didn't want to talk about writing, the famous writer Ken Kesey said. Writing was obsolete. Instead, he was going to talk about an extra-terrestrial conspiracy.

The famous writer Ken Kesey said he believed humankind was basically good. He knew more nice people than people he thought not so nice. He assumed history could confirm his observation. For thousands and thousands of years, he maintained, humanity had been trying to reach perfection. There were the arts, the sciences, indoor plumbing: all good things. Yet with all good things came evil. Aristotle's principles of rhetoric allowed Hitler to invade Poland, the Spanish Inquisition sprang from a selfless philosophy of universal fraternity, Pasteur's germ theory caused a terrifying population explosion: all good intentions somehow messed up. Thousands of years of human evolution had succeeded in getting us to a point where a handful of shitheads could reduce all human accomplishments to crazy careening atoms with the push of a few buttons. This was progress? Was humanity really so stupid? So ineffectual? So inherently brutish?

The famous writer Ken Kesey thought not. Humans loved beauty, loved life, loved goodness, loved truth, loved love.

It was the Venusians that were fucking us up.

For over ten thousand years now, he claimed, Venusian agents had been infiltrating the corpus of humanity in an attempt to fashion evil out of all man-made good. The planet Venus was uncomfortably muggy and depressing, he said, ten times worse than Baltimore in August. The Venusians planned to have humanity kill itself off so that they could take over our lovely temperate planet. They were patient, he said, as well as clever. They could make themselves look just like us. No one could be sure that the person sitting next to him or her wasn't a diabolically disguised Venusian patiently planning that person's demise or, worse, that person's instrumental role in the demise of countless others. Many college students turned to their neighbors with mock horror. I did too.

But there was a way to identify a Venusian agent, the famous writer said. As we all knew, every human had an aura, an electrical discharge that was scientifically perceptible through certain new photographic techniques. Even without the use of these techniques, one human can sense another human's aura with what we call our sixth sense, our extra sense, in much the same way that a dog can sense whether a person approaches it with friendly or malign intent. And that is how a human can tell when he or she is in the presence of a Venusian.

Venusians have no auras.

And the lack of an aura, Kesey claimed, could be subtly perceived through the wispiest feeling that something was not right about somebody, through the hint of a premonition. Thus it was that if a human were walking down the street and saw somebody who for some reason gave that human a bad feeling, that human could be sure the person responsible for that bad feeling was not, in fact, a fellow human. That person was certainly a Venusian. And the only hope for the human race lay in identifying all Venusian agents and doing away with them.

The famous writer Ken Kesey called on the assembly to join hearts, hands, and auras in an attempt to ascertain whether there were any Venusian agents hiding among the gathering. Since Venusians had no auras, they obviously could not join auras with ours, and so could be recognized for what they truly were: nonhuman.

Everybody joined hands. I did too. The famous writer led our aura-strengthening meditations. Om, he said. Om. Om. Ooohhmmmmmmm. There were no agents among us, thank God. We represented the pure core of humankind. The famous writer Ken Kesey concluded his talk by calling on each human in the assembly to beware of and constantly on guard against the Venusian threat. Everyone applauded. I did too.

Afterwards, I approached him. "Inspirational," I said.

"Thanks, bub," he said. "It's my newest goof."

"Good goof," I said. "When are you coming out with another book? It's been quite a while."

He stared off over my shoulder, told me he was burnt out on writing. "Too limiting, too many rules, not enough precision," he said. "You can never say exactly what you mean."

I wondered what he meant.

"Syntax is based in logic," he said. "But logic can't explain its own basis, which is exactly what needs explaining most. I'm into extra-sensory transmission now."

"Sounds like half-baked trippy bullshit to me," I said.

The famous writer Ken Kesey gave me that lazy half grin of his. "Thanks for noticing," he said. "So what's *your* latest? Been a long time between goofs for you, ain't it?"

"I'm done with that," I said.

"You? Never."

"Me. Forever." I pulled out the two rubber-banded manila envelopes I'd been toting around in my backpack, handed the package to him.

He sniffed it, coughed. "What's this?"

"This is yours," I said. "It needs your special touch."

Then I told him something about it. When I'd finished, he eyed me skeptically. "You're crazy as a cuckoo."

"Not yet. Just give it a chance, will you?"

"Well fuck me with a ballpeen hammer," he drawled, leaning back and thumbing his nose, "I'll look at it, bub. Just because you sound crazier than me. No promises."

Then he winged his way off to the cradle of civilization. And what can I say? How say it?

Yes, yes, certainly: imagination yields madness; madness consists of that which can't be communicated. Be careful now. The trick is simply to report, to tell, to subordinate imagination to a single-minded rendition of the facts.

Just the facts.

It's incredibly important to imagine *nothing*.

•

It all starts one muggy evening late in June 1978 at Emily and Gardner Jones's third-floor apartment on 101st Street just off West End Ave. Emily sits in the living room dressed in terrycloth shorts and halter, her long, lean, fashionable body glowing with perspiration. The apartment has no air conditioning, and Gardner's got the only fan whirring in the study where he's busy working on the second chapter of his projected novel Touched by the Hand of the Universal Committee. Emily sits sweating, listening to the muffled tickety-tick of typing from the next room, trying to concentrate on proofreading Gardner's first chapter. So far, in ten minutes of reading, she hasn't managed to make it past the first page. It's just too hot to read. Still, it must be done. Gardner's editor says if he doesn't see some results pretty soon, Gardner can kiss any future advances goodbye.

This is the first thing Gardner's done in over a year, the first story he's become excited about since he finished his *Dreams Trilogy*. His first novel, *After the Dreams Began*, was an immediate success and made him a prodigy in the science fiction community at the age of twenty-three. His second, *All Dreams Gone to the Corner for a Pack of Smokes*, was equally successful and tended to dissipate certain fears that the first was a fluke. His third, *Return of the Dreams*, capped off the series and gave him a Nebula Award for best trilogy. But the glory's faded now. He hasn't done much since. Sure, he writes every day, but he hasn't been able to finish anything he considers worthwhile. Fears he's used himself up. But then last week the idea for this novel came together, and he's been working non-stop ever since. Like a man possessed.

A drop of sweat rolls from Emily's forehead down the bridge of her nose, drips *plash* in the center of the first page. She hasn't been getting much work done lately either. Paints and canvas collect dust in the hall closet. Too busy catering to Gardner. She brushes a wet strand of hair from her eyes, concentrates on the first sentence again.

```
Poor, silly, uninformed humans, to imagine
that something as intricate and complex as
an entire universe could possibly make its
own rules, establish its own existence, and
maintain its function for eons upon eons, all
by its very own mindless self.
```

Silence pulls Emily's eyes from the page.

Gardner's stopped typing. The door to the study opens. Gardner glares at her.

"Well?" he says.

"Well what?" Emily says.

"Are you going to get it?"

"Get what?"

Gardner curses, strides across the room to where she sits, grabs the phone from the end table next to her. "Hello?" he says. "Hello? Hello!" He slams down the receiver. "I'm sick of this. It's been happening all week. I run to the phone, but whoever's calling hangs up when I answer."

Emily tilts her head. "What are you talking about? The phone didn't ring."

"It happened twice while you were out shopping. I pick up the phone in the middle of a ring and all I get is a dial tone."

"But the phone didn't ring."

"It really throws me off my work. I'm rolling along on a great idea, the words are coming faster than I can type them, and then that goddamn phone starts ringing and there's nobody there when I answer. It's maddening. We probably have our lines crossed or something. How about calling Ma Bell and telling them to fix it?"

Emily shakes her head. "I'm trying to tell you. I was sitting right here. The phone didn't ring."

Gardner stares blankly. "When?"

"Just now."

Gardner rolls his eyes, says he knows it didn't ring just now. It rang just a moment ago, just before he answered it. Emily reaches up, grabs his wrists, tells him patiently, so patiently, that no, it didn't ring then either. She laughs. He's working too hard, she says. He's got bells ringing in the belfry. The phone hasn't rung the whole time she's been sitting here.

Gardner pulls away from her. "And what difference does that make?" he says. "There's still nobody there when I answer. Do you know how irritating that is? I can't be jumping up every five minutes to answer the phone when nobody's even calling."

Emily stares at him. "You're really nuts," she says.

Gardner draws himself up, stands tall, dark, and frowning before her, says the least she could do is try to keep him from being interrupted by annoying phone calls when nobody's even calling and she's sitting right there next to the phone while he's busy working in the next room. How about a little consideration, huh?

Emily leans forward. A little preoccupation, a touch of absent-mindedness can be endearing; but this is too much. "Listen to yourself," she says. "You're telling me to answer the phone when nobody's there."

"Is that asking too much?" says Gardner. "I'll never finish this book if I keep getting interrupted. We can't live on the advance forever, you know, and your work isn't exactly raking in the cash."

Emily's jaw twitches. Sore subject. Her last show, "Dyslexic Anima: Visions of Women in the City," was critically acclaimed

153

by most of the important art reviewers, but for some reason, hardly any of her pieces sold. She blamed the gallery for persuading her to price them too high. She has since started on a new project, one that has her roaming Times Square with camera in hand, taking preliminary photos of the many so-called "bag ladies" who live on the streets and in the alleyways, but it will be some time before this one can pay off, if it ends up paying off at all. It's a study in depression, desperation, and loss, and she's not sure she'll be able to pull off painting exactly what she sees.

But that's the artist's job, Emily knows: to continually strive, though you arrive at nothing but doubt.

Emily takes a deep breath, rubs her eyes. "It's too hot," she says. "You win. From now on, I'll answer the phone when it's not ringing."

"That's all I ask," Gardner says. He leans down, plants a humid kiss on Emily's forehead. "I don't mean to be a dick," he says. "It's just I have a lot of work to do. This novel is driving me crazy." He returns to his study, closes the door behind him.

Emily stares after him. Sometimes it seems like Gardner puts his mind on automatic pilot: it just flies around without knowing quite where it's going. She sighs, goes back to the task at hand. She reads the first sentence of the manuscript again, goes on to the second.

```
Of course, that's the way humans have
been conditioned to think; it causes fewer
problems for the creatures who really run
the show.
```

On to the third, fourth, fifth sentences. She turns the page, pencils in a correct spelling, slashes a typo, turns the page, continues reading.

Gardner's first chapter introduces a young science fiction writer named Kissan Roy who gets an idea for a novel about a young science fiction writer named Muzhikov Smirnov who's writing a short story about a young space traveler in the Inter-Galactic Corps of Engineers named Hortelano Garcia who, blown off course in his one-person warp-drive reconnaissance vessel by a quasar storm, ends up falling helplessly through a space-time flux, coming to rest finally in an uncharted cross-dimensional galaxy, his ship badly damaged. Garcia puts down on the nearest planet for repairs only to discover a strange race of alien beings.

```
They resembled spherical blobs of translucent
lime Jell-O supported by a tripod of stork-
like legs. Three symmetrically positioned
triple-jointed appendages grew from the upper
hemisphere of the torso. Three long, supple,
triple-jointed digits grew from the joint
closest to the body. Thousands of flagella-
like "feelers" sprouted like fine green hair
from the second joint. The final joint, or
"wrist," sported three seemingly vestigial
talons. Their heads had three faces, each
dominated by three triple-faceted eyes that
made it appear that the creatures could see
in all directions simultaneously.
```

Hortelano Garcia learns that the Triple People, as he comes to calls them, have translated all of the universe's phenomena into a base three system. This system would prove indecipherable to humans, but its integers might be freely translated as Yes, No, and Maybe. The feelers are used for communication, which is accomplished through a combination of each of the feelers transmitting or receiving its integer in an orchestrated sequence with thousands of other feelers.

Of course, Hortelano Garcia doesn't discover all of this on his own. The Triple People are able to communicate with him telepathically. Thus he comes to realize that this is a race of truly superior and vastly intelligent beings. He requests that they help him repair his spaceship, but, surprisingly, they refuse. Garcia demands to know the reason for their refusal. They refuse to explain. Garcia realizes that he is virtually a prisoner of the Triple People and vows to escape or know the reason why.

Muzhikov Smirnov is half-finished with his story about the adventure of Hortelano Garcia, has just come to the point where Garcia will discover the true reason for his captivity, when inexplicably he runs into the dreaded writer's block. He can't seem to put the words together correctly. They don't say precisely what he wants them to. Smirnov spends hours in front of his typewriter staring at the blank page, reading over his work until it begins to make no sense whatsoever. He smokes too much, drinks too much, fights with his wife. He starts talking to himself, answers himself when his self talks to him. He begins to fear that he's losing his mind; still, he refuses to give up on his story.

Here, Gardner has Kissan Roy, the primary narrator of Gardner's new book, narrate the reason for Muzhikov Smirnov's problem. In writing about a character who inadvertently stumbles upon a race of truly superior and vastly intelligent beings, Roy explains, Smirnov himself has inadvertently stumbled upon a near-perfect description of a real race of beings who are unbelievably more truly superior and more vastly intelligent than good old Smirnov could ever begin to imagine. They are, in effect, gods. They are, in fact, responsible for the creation of the universe. They are, in toto, the sum and source of each and every millirem of the universe's energy; they control, direct, and maintain its flow.

Cause and effect, bound and rebound, push and be pushed: nothing, Kissan Roy insists, happens by chance. From a star gone brilliantly nova to a sunny day in May gone bleak with the threat of rain to a faithful husband and provider gone to the corner for a pack of smokes never to return—everything has been planned in advance, put into existence, and carefully watched over by the beings our man Kissan calls the Universal Organizational Committee.

Why does the Committee do what it does? Neither Roy nor Smirnov will presume to explain the Committee's primary motive, but Roy muses that our creators are a tidy race, driven by an infinite sense of ennui combined with an inexhaustible penchant for law and order. For whatever reason they do what they do, the Committee does it well. They do it efficiently. They do it with style and class and apparent ease.

And they do it incognito.

Gardner has Kissan Roy explain that the Committee has created billions of life forms throughout the grand reaches of the universe, and that these life forms have been created and watched over in such a way that not one of them can ever guess the true nature if its origin. Too much self-knowledge on the part of any of these created forms would toss an unplanned, unknown, immeasurable variable into the universal equation, subjecting it to an eventual breakdown and ultimate chaos.

And so far everything's gone according to plan. None of the created life forms has come close to discovering where it originally came from. Almost none. None with the possible exception of one.

Gardner writes that when Roy writes Smirnov writing Garcia describing a nearly spot-on physical description that matches that of the Committee, the Committee begins to worry. Who knows what this human will imagine next? Of course, Gardner's demi-level hero Muzhikov Smirnov has only come up with a very limited description. He describes only one aspect of the Committee, the form they use to act in only one of an infinity of dimensions. In other dimensions, they look nothing like Smirnov's description; mainly because in most dimensions the Committee doesn't "look" like anything to humans, since humanity lacks the senses necessary to perceive anything in dimensions outside its own.

Still, the Committee is worried, if you can imagine the creators of the universe worrying at all. A mistake has been made, the Committee realizes. Somewhere amid the planning, engineering, and/or maintenance functions that keep the universe universal, a variable hasn't been accounted for. This human Muzhikov Smirnov has been allowed to visualize the smallest fraction of what the universe is truly about. And that mistake cannot go uncorrected. Mistakes have a way of multiplying.

Now the Committee could simply kill Smirnov, or even make it so Smirnov never existed at all. The creators have a lot of tricks up their sleeves. But they'd rather not eradicate Smirnov. Too flashy. Too messy. Too inordinate an allocation of energy for such a small job. Instead, the Committee has decided to simply drive him crazy so he'll never be able to imagine anything that will make any kind of sense to the rest of humanity ever again. The writer's block is just a start. Making him talk to himself gets the process rolling. They have other goodies in store for good old Muzhikov Smirnov as well.

Towards the end of Gardner's first chapter, Kissan Roy is just beginning the third chapter of his novel in which he plans to explain just what these other goodies are, when the strange phone calls start.

All day long: ring, ring, ring. And when Roy answers it, all he gets is a dial tone. His wife swears she doesn't hear it ringing. Ma Bell says it's in perfect working order. This goes on for days. And just as our cosmic tour guide Kissan Roy begins to think that perhaps he should have his ears checked, his trusty Labrador retriever Maya tells him he's working too hard, give it a rest.

Maybe he should take a break from that crazy novel and go on a little vacay, Maya says.

Kissan Roy nods at the dog. Maybe Maya's right. And then it hits him. He is going crazy. What if he himself, like his character Muzhikov Smirnov and Smirnov's character Hortelano Garcia, has accidentally stumbled upon the true state of affairs in the universe? What if there really is something like the Committee? What if there really is a flaw in the Committee's design that allowed him to imagine its existence? What if right now something like his invented Committee were trying to correct that flaw?

Is it possible?

Maya says don't be silly, but Kissan Roy becomes convinced it's true. He fears for his sanity. Still, he vows he'll finish this novel or go crazy trying. He'll be damned if some lousy superior beings somewhere get away with tampering with his artistic impulses.

Oh, but the phone makes it so difficult to concentrate. He takes it off the hook, and still it rings. He rips the cord from the wall, and still it rings. His wife threatens to have him committed if he doesn't stop acting so crazy, and he screams at her to leave him alone. He tries to ignore the ringing, but it's so insistent, so loud, so unavoidably *there* every time he tries to think that he finds himself constantly anticipating the next ring instead of thinking about his novel. It's getting to the point where he can hardly think at *all* any more.

Kissan Roy is at his wit's end.

•

Thus ends Gardner's first chapter.

Emily straightens the manuscript, sets it on the end table. So far... *meh*. She can't imagine where it's going to go from here, and she finds it hard to believe that science fiction fans will go for last season's trendy postmodern writer writing about a writer writing about a writer deal. She won't mention it to Gardner—he's obviously obsessed with the idea—but this particular flavor of literary self-awareness was branded self-indulgence by most literary critics years ago. God only knows what the average adolescent sci-fi reader would make of it.

At least the chapter explains Gardner's strange behavior with the phone. Obviously, he thought she'd already read it, thought he was being cute acting out one of its scenes. Emily feels bad for becoming so irritated with him.

She looks at the phone next to her. It's not ringing. Her eyes crease with mischief. She picks up the receiver.

"Never mind, Gardner," she calls. "I got it."

Typing stops. "Got what?" Gardner shouts.

Emily giggles. "The phone. It wasn't ringing so I answered it. Nobody was calling."

The study door bangs open. "What is *wrong* with you?" Gardner rages. "I'm trying to work and you're playing games."

Emily's smile fades.

"I told you a hundred times not to interrupt me," Gardner says.

"I know," Emily says. "But I just read that part—"

"I don't care *what* you just read." Gardner's dark eyes blaze. "I don't have time to hear about it."

Emily closes her eyes. She can't deal with him when he shouts. "Sorry," she says. "It won't happen again."

"Great! That's all I ask." He slams the door behind him. Typing resumes, stops again. "*Just leave me alone!*" he bellows.

Emily pulls her long, damp hair into a pile on top of her head, prays for a breeze to dry the back of her neck, frowns. Gardner can be such an asshole sometimes. Especially when he's writing. She can usually handle his idiosyncrasies, moods, fits of temper. But not this evening. It's just too hot.

•

Tuesday nights Emily teaches an intro drawing course in the noncredit Community Arts Program at Columbia. After class, she meets with her friend Pat Rushin, a tenure-track assistant prof in Columbia's English Department who teaches a graduate creative writing workshop at the same time right down the hall from her.

"You look like I could use a drink," he tells her.

"Absolutely," Emily says.

"My chairman says I gotta try the Old King Cole at the St. Regis. They make a specialty drink called a Red Snapper that's supposed to be killer."

Emily rolls her eyes. "It's just an overpriced Bloody Mary, and we're *not* doing midtown."

Rushin is a sparesly published fictioneer whose tenuous claim to literary legitimacy consists of a handful of painstakingly minimalist short stories published in a handful of little literary magazines and a single "critical" essay that introduced the world of letters to the School of Non-textual Literary Criticism.. He earned his M.A. in Creative Writing from Baltimore's Johns Hopkins Writing Seminars, where he studied under the famed postmodern maximalist John Barth, who wrote in his minimalist letter of recommendation to Columbia, "Although Rushin is not prolific, he is an earnest writer and a thoroughly charming young man who deserves your every consideration."

So with Emily's veto of midtown madness, she and Rushin end up just off campus as usual, sitting at the bar toward the back of the Lion's Head Tavern.

Rushin sips the foam off his second draft. Emily stares into her first scotch on the rocks, strangely silent.

"Why so glum?" Rushin says.

Emily takes a long gulp of her drink, turns on her stool to face him. "Listen," she says, "I can talk to you, right?"

"Right."

"You know what I'm talking about when I talk to you, right?"

"Mostly."

"I'm worried," she says. "I think Gardner's going crazy."

"Leave the bum," Rushin nods. "Come live with me. Problem solved. No worries."

Emily grabs his hand, squeezes hard. "I'm serious, Pat."

Rushin looks at his hand in hers. His face colors, camouflages the rash of freckles across his cheeks, blends nicely with his curly red hair. Emily releases his hand. Rushin smiles, fishes in his pocket for a cigarette.

Emily has to watch it with Rushin. A month after they met, she had a short affair with him. They went to bed together exactly twice before she called it off. It was nice, nothing special, more like two kids playing doctor than a man and a woman making serious love, but she felt guilty about being unfaithful to Gardner and not sufficiently attracted to Rushin to swallow her guilt. Rushin agreed it couldn't work. He felt guilty, too, he told her. They ended it like adults: no regrets.

Still, now and then after she's had a few drinks, and especially when things aren't going well with Gardner, Emily finds herself looking at Rushin with more than simple friendship in her eyes, and she can't help feeling he's returning that look.

She has to watch herself.

Emily ducks her head. "Look, I don't want to sound melodramatic, but I'm serious. Gardner acts like a crazy man."

Rushin nods, sips his beer. "How long has this been going on?"

"A couple of weeks, maybe. Ever since he started working on his novel. I think the novel's driving him crazy."

Rushin shrugs. "Possible. What's it about?"

So for the next ten minutes Emily gives Rushin a synopsis of Gardner's first chapter, along with her rendition of the telephone scene.

"God," Rushin says when she's finished. "Save us from artsy science fiction writers. What am I killing myself for writing serious fiction?"

Actually, Rushin had never "killed himself" writing any kind of anything. What landed him the plum Columbia gig when Hopkins grad school fellows were scrambling for poverty-level wages teaching frosh comp at community colleges turned out to be an essay entitled "Undue Influence: The Hegemony of the Primary Text in American Literary Criticism." He'd knocked off the first draft in a single inebriated sitting. Tongue surgically implanted in cheek, Rushin argued that since quantum theory was beginning to prove that nothing in our view of "reality" was necessarily "real," the text itself offered little more than a critic's subliminally biased view of meaning. It was a pure grad school goof inspired by a workshop in which a fellow student had the temerity to say to John Barth, when asked his opinion of the story under discussion, "Well, Jack, I didn't actually have time to read it, but from what everyone else is saying, I have to agree that Sandra's characterization of the Bishop's housekeeper probably borders on cliché."

Voila! The School of Non-Textual Criticism was born.

Rushin cleaned up the manuscript and mailed it off to *The North American Review*, whose editor had sent him some encouraging rejections of his fiction. As dumb luck would have it, "Undue Influence" was published in *NAR*'s next issue, and as even dumber luck dictated, several cutting-edge critics, while mindful it was meant as a satire, unaccountably took the essay's precepts seriously enough to ignite a vehemently studious debate in English departments across the country, culminating in *NAR*'s special issue the following year, "The Emperor's Old Nudity: Literary Criticism Unclothed," making Rushin's essay eminently citable and his name instantly recognizable to the intelligentsia in Columbia's English Department.

"Gardner will sell that trash, too," he's complaining now. "I work my ass off trying to make meaningful art, and nobody reads it. The serious writer gets no respect."

Emily rolls her eyes. She's heard this song before. "Gardner's a way serious writer," she says. "That's the problem. He's obsessed. He's in the study typing like a madman on the second chapter most of the day. He hardly even talks to me, and when he does, he says something crazy. I'm really worried about him, Pat!"

Rushin pats her hand ineffectually. "Look, it's probably nothing serious. He's just caught up in his work. He's playing, that's all. So he answers the phone when it doesn't ring, so what? That's not crazy, it's just silly."

"It's more than that," Emily says.

"What? You expect him to go on a killing spree or something?"

Emily grabs his hand, squeezes hard. Rushin winces.

"Don't," Emily says. "Don't you treat me like some neurotic chick. Not you, Pat. You know better. You haven't been living with the man. You don't know what he's been like. Sure he's caught up in his story. He's so caught up, he can't tell reality from fiction." She lets go of his hand. "Order us a couple more drinks. This is going to take a while. Now *listen.*"

•

Case in point.

On the day following Gardner's telephone episode, Emily's sitting at the kitchen table typing up the corrected first chapter. She comes to a word that she circled while proofing, since she wasn't sure of the spelling then and hadn't a dictionary handy. The dictionary is in the study.

She enters the study quietly, sees Gardner at his desk, elbows propped on either side of his typewriter, face buried in his hands. He does not look up.

Careful not to disturb him while he's busy thinking, Emily crosses the room on tiptoe, reaches for the dictionary on the bookshelf behind him.

"Give it up," Gardner says.

Emily turns around. Gardner hasn't moved.

"Go to hell," he says. "I'll finish this thing if it kills me."

"What?" Emily says.

"There's no way," Gardner says. "They won't *let* me."

Emily pulls the dictionary from the shelf, hugs it to her chest.

"Let them try to stop me," Gardner says. "It's too late now."

Emily touches Gardner's shoulder. "What?" she says.

Gardner lowers his hands slowly, looks up at her. Blurred eyes focus. "What what?" he says.

"What did you say?"

Gardner's brow furrows. "I said 'What what?'"

"No, before that."

"Was I saying something?"

"Yes. You said a lot of things."

Gardner looks away. "Just talking to myself, I guess."

Emily frowns. "Are you doing this on purpose, or what?"

"What do you mean?"

"I mean you never talk to yourself and now all of a sudden you're talking to yourself. What's the story?"

"No story," Gardner says. He leans back, rubs his hands through his hair.

Emily touches his back and he shivers. He looks so haggard: baggy eyes hang down over creased, puffy face. She massages tense neck muscles.

"You need some rest," she says. "You've been working too hard."

Gardner's broad back goes rigid. "You too," he says. "Now *you're* trying to stop me."

Emily backs away. "Gardner, I'm just—"

Gardner slams his fist on the desk. "Leave me alone," he says, face twisted, eyes glazed. "Just get out of here."

Emily flees the room, dictionary clutched tight in trembling hands.

•

Later in the week, Emily returns from an appointment with Dr. Valerie Kopanski, Gardner's old analyst. She treated Gardner for a series of panic attacks he suffered while working on the final book in his trilogy, but once the book was published, the attacks ceased, and he quit analysis. When Emily told Dr. Kopanski she was actually there to discuss Gardner's mental stability, the good doctor brusquely informed her that patient confidentiality dictated that Gardner would have to come in for his own appointment. "But we can talk about what you're going through, dear." After listening to Emily's tearful rendition of Gardner's recent behavior, Dr. Kopanski grudgingly opined that it sounded like he was once again reacting to the stress of his artistic doubts, acting out to mask a neurotic fear of creative impotence, and that Gardner should visit her so they could discuss this relapse in depth. In the meantime she could prescribe Valium for Emily to help her cope with any further episodes.

At the third floor landing, Emily bumps into a frantic Mrs. Fronista, the lady who lives across the hall from them, who asks her if she's seen her toy terrier Fidel. Mrs. Fronista left her apartment door open to catch a little breeze from the stairwell, and, apparently, Fidel's run off.

"I hope nobody kidnapped him," Mrs. Fronista says. "They do that, you know. Kidnap dogs and make them fight in warehouses in Brooklyn. I read it in the paper."

Emily assures her there's probably little demand for gladiatorial toy terriers, tells her she'll keep an eye out for him.

As she enters the living room, Emily hears Gardner in the study. Talking. Jesus, not again. Gardner's voice rises. "Tell your people they can't touch me!" he's yelling. "They can't stop me!"

Emily opens the door. Gardner crouches in the middle of the room holding a whimpering Fidel roughly by the collar. Emily slams the door behind her. Surprised, Gardner releases Fidel who immediately runs to Emily and licks her shoes.

"Gardner, what are you doing?"

"I'll kill that goddamn dog!" Gardner shouts.

"Gardner, you're acting like a madman!"

Gardner flinches. His face pales. He sits heavily on the floor. "I know," he says softly. He raises pleading eyes. "Emily, that dog's been talking to me."

"Cut it out. That's straight out of your book. Why are you acting like this?"

"I'm not acting. It's true."

Emily looks at him. His face is drawn, white; his lower lip twitches. "Listen, don't get mad," she says. "I really think you need a break. You're working so hard you don't know what's going on anymore. I'm worried about you."

Gardner chuckles weakly, rolls onto his back. "That's just what Fidel told me out in the hall when I went to get the mail. 'Trabajas demasiado, mi amigo,' he told me. '¿Por qué no se toma una pequeña siesta?'"

"I didn't know you spoke Spanish."

"I don't," Gardner says dully. "Fidel does."

Emily kneels next to him, lays a hand on his chest. "I went to see Valerie Kopanski today. I made an appointment for you. She'll see you next Wednesday."

"You think I'm going crazy?"

"I don't know what to think. That's why I want you to see her."

Gardner rolls his head back and forth. "She can't help me. Nobody can help me. They're trying to get me, Emily."

"Who's trying to get you?"

Gardner blinks. "The Committee."

She clutches his arm. "It's a story, Gardner. It's not real."

Gardner's laughter sounds like a bark. "Just because it's a story doesn't mean it can't be real. I've come up with something that somebody somewhere never expected anybody to come up with." He raises his head suddenly. "Do you hear the phone ringing?"

Emily catches her breath. "No."

"I didn't think so." He lays his head down.

Emily begins to cry. "You're driving me crazy," she sobs.

Gardner hugs her to him, strokes her back, tells her it's okay, he's sorry, don't cry. Emily wipes her tears, sits up.

"Will you see Dr. Kopanski next week?"

Gardner promises he will.

"Will you try to get some rest, take a break from working?"

Gardner acquiesces. She's right, he tells her, he has been working too hard. His head's filled with this novel. He sits up next to her, asks if there's any beer in the fridge. Emily says sit tight, she'll get it. She goes to the kitchen. When she returns, Gardner's at his desk staring at his typewriter.

"Gardner, you said."

Gardner looks up. "Said what?" he says. "Do me a favor, get that dog out of here. I can't work with him watching me."

•

Gardner's been good. He's still working on his novel, yes, but he's acting relatively normal again. Monday evening Emily walks in on him while he's writing and he doesn't even blow up. She suggests he call it a day, maybe they can go out to eat. Gardner's too tired to go out, but he agrees to quit working. Maybe he'll just poke around the kitchen, grab a sandwich, watch a little TV tonight. That's fine with Emily; she can use the study to catch up on her own work.

Emily gets her drawing pad and pencils, settles herself in Gardner's swivel chair. Through the door to the living room, she can hear the tinny whisper of television violence: miniature car crashes, sirens, gunshots. She gets up and turns on the fan. Soon she's hard at work sketching from pictures she took of those Times Square bag ladies last month.

Some time later she's completed her preliminary sketches. Maybe she'll have time tomorrow to do something with them in acrylics. She stands, stretches, looks at the clock. After midnight. She yawns, turns off the fan, notices how quiet it is. Gardner must have gone to bed. She turns off the light and walks into the living room.

It's dark. And there on the floor, back propped against the sofa, sits Gardner.

"Oh," Emily says. "You're still up."

A nearly full moon hangs low in the sky, shines through the bay window, makes Gardner's face glow pale and expressionless.

"I'm going to bed," Emily says. "What are you doing?"

Gardner stares straight ahead. "Watching TV."

Emily nods. "Gardner, the television isn't turned on."

"I know. I turned it off."

"Then why are you still watching it?"

Gardner's line of vision doesn't waver. "It's interesting."

Emily shakes her head. Eccentric? Sure. But she's tired. Not in the mood to deal with him. He'll be seeing Valerie Kopanski in a couple of days. Let *her* deal with him.

"Goodnight," she says, but Gardner's too wrapped up in what he's watching to answer.

Later, Emily awakens, sits up in bed alone. The clock says 3:50. She gets up, goes to the living room. Gardner still sits staring.

"Gardner," she whispers. "What are you doing?"

His voice is low and faraway. "Watching TV."

Emily switches on a lamp, stands above him. "Come to bed."

Gardner doesn't even blink. "I will," he says. "As soon as this thing is over."

"What thing?"

"This thing I'm watching."

Emily stoops, touches his arm. The skin is cool. "Gardner, tell me, please, what do you think you're watching?"

"TV," Gardner says.

"What do you *see*?"

Gardner's face looks like a mug shot of a paper doll. "You can't imagine," he says.

Emily slumps to the floor, rolls up against him. He doesn't budge. She pounds the floor, but he doesn't notice. She sits up, tries to tickle him. He doesn't feel. She follows his gaze to the blank screen, looks back at him, shrugs.

"Mind if I join you?" she says.

No answer. Gardner minds nothing. She cuddles next to him, stares at the blank tube. "This is so romantic," she says. "I should have made popcorn."

•

Rushin laughs, lifts his empty mug. The bartender brings him another beer.

"I know," says Emily. "It's the kind of thing you don't want to take seriously, because if you do, it's not funny anymore. It's scary. I sat next to him like that for an hour. He never moved a muscle. And his eyes. He was really *looking* at something, but there was nothing there but a blank screen.

171

It got spooky. Finally, I jumped up and turned on the TV. A John Wayne western was showing. Gardner still kept staring at it, like nothing had changed. I sat on top of him and started screaming and punching him. Is that crazy?"

Rushin shrugs, sips his beer.

"Anyway, all of a sudden he starts having these convulsions. His eyes rolled up and he was growling and kicking. I didn't know what to do. I just hugged him as hard as I could. That lasted about a minute. Then he calmed down and opened his eyes and asked me to turn down the TV. He didn't want to wake the neighbors, he said. I turned off the television. Then he started stretching and yawning like he just woke up. He told me I wouldn't believe what he just saw. I said what. He said infinity. Just a little piece of it, just the ass-end, he said, but it was beyond anything I could ever imagine. I said I didn't know we could pick up infinity on our set. He laughed. He was in a good mood. He said the Committee beamed it in live from the center of the universe. I thought I'd better humor him, so I asked what infinity looked like. He said it didn't *look* like anything. He said infinity's the marriage of countless variable dimensions in a state of continual flux. Exactly."

Emily finishes her drink in one swallow.

"He looked so pleased with himself. He kept saying he'd taken the Committee's best shot, that they couldn't touch him any harder, that the Committee probably thought a vision of everything there is would drive him crazy, but all it had done was make him stronger. He knew how to deal with the Committee now, he said. He went to bed then, but I told him I wanted to watch the rest of the movie. The truth is, I was afraid to go to bed with him. I slept on the sofa with the television on. I woke up early and left the house without waking him."

Rushin stares at her. Emily rubs her eyes. "I don't know what to do," she says.

"I don't know what to tell you," Rushin says. "Except you don't have to go back there if you don't want to. Really, you can have my bed. I'll sleep on the floor."

Emily's shoulders sag. Rushin puts an arm around her. She leans against him.

"I can't leave him alone," she says. "He scares me, but I'm scared for him, too. He's going to do something really crazy, and I don't want to be there alone when he does it. Could you come home with me, Pat, hang around a while so I don't have to deal with him alone?"

Rushin says sure thing. They settle the tab, hail a cab, and off they go to see just how crazy Gardner really is.

•

Emily's key unlocks the door, but Gardner's got the deadbolt snapped shut. She rings the bell. Waits. Rings again. Waits. Rings. Fidgets. Rings and rings and rings.

"God, I knew it," she says. "He killed himself."

Rushin stands to the side as she pounds at the door.

Finally, the bolt slides, door opens, and there stands Gardner clad only in a pair of plaid boxers, smiling, healthy, and rippling with muscles.

"Where have you been?" he says.

"Where have you been. I rang a skabillion times."

He bends to kiss her. "You taste like scotch."

She sniffs. "Have you been smoking?"

Gardner gives her a wounded look. "You know I quit."

"Yeah," Emily says, brushing past him. "Repeatedly."

Rushin follows her in.

"Pat, good to see you." Gardner grabs Rushin's hand,

pumps it. "Sorry to make you wait. Haven't been too good at answering bells lately. Busy, busy, busy. How's the academic treadmill?" Gardner talks in a burst of animated good humor, wraps an arm around Rushin's shoulders, pulls him towards the living room, plops next to him on the sofa.

Emily sits in the rocking chair across from them, watching Gardner lean on Rushin and catch up on small talk. Pat always seems a little intimidated by Gardner. She's assured him before that Gardner knows nothing about the affair they had; still, whenever she sees the two together, she notices that Gardner tends to back Pat into a corner with his aggressive style. Even though the two are nearly the same size—Gardner's only an inch taller, maybe ten pounds heavier—Gardner seems to dwarf Pat. Gardner's like that with a lot of people: he takes up space, tends to impose himself on what most people consider *their* space.

Gardner's all hyped and jumpy, leaning into Rushin, edging him towards the end of the sofa, waving one arm and touching Rushin's knee, arm, shoulder with the other. He's been working like a dog on this novel, he's saying.

Rushin crosses his legs, folds his hands in his lap. "So how's it coming?" he says.

Gardner leans closer. "Between you and me, Pat, I've had some trouble with it. I imagine Emily's told you how crazy I've been."

Rushin fumbles. "No. Not really. I mean, you know."

"Hey, it's okay," Gardner says. He grabs Rushin's knee, squeezes. I *have* been acting crazy. But that's over now. I finished the second chapter today. I'm over the hump."

"Good. Can't wait to see it."

"Great," Gardner says, jumping to his feet. "I'm dying to show somebody."

"Gardner," Emily says.

"I want you to see it, too, Emily." He walks over to her, grabs the arms of her chair, rocks her back. "The Committee gave me a lot of trouble for awhile, but everything's fine now."

Emily glances at Rushin.

Gardner's eyes dance. "The thing is, you can't have creatures with unlimited powers. You have to give them some kind of weakness so humanity has a chance of fighting back. That's what I came up with today. Humanity's chance. The Committee's weakness. The thing is, the Committee made everything there is, and they *see* everything there is all across space and time. But they're blind to anything they didn't create. They can't see what *could* be." He winks. "No fucking imagination. That's their flaw. Hang on! I'll show you!"

And he's off to the study.

Emily looks at Rushin.

Rushin shrugs. "Sounds mostly okay to me," he whispers. "Like, you know, a passionate writer immersed in his work?"

Maybe so, Emily thinks. Maybe Gardner's pushed fiction out of his life and back into his novel where it belongs. Still, he seems too manic. Too high, too happy, too soon.

Gardner returns, sits next to Rushin, hands him the manuscript. "Check this out."

Rushin looks at it, squints, looks at the second page. "I don't…" he starts, trails off.

"It's a little rough," Gardner says. "Full of typos."

Rushin turns a page, looks up. "I don't get it."

Gardner claps his hands suddenly. Rushin flinches.

"I forgot," says Gardner. "That's the second chapter. You haven't read the first one yet. Wait a second." He jumps up, goes back to the study.

Rushin leafs through the manuscript, mouth tight. Emily gets up, sits beside him. He gives her the manuscript, shakes his head.

CHAPTER TWO

```
+++--+-+/ /-/+++-/++ +--/++---/-++ --/+--+
+++/-+-+++/ --+++------+/-- ++/-+++-++++/-
-/+ -+--+/- +++-+/-+ +/-/++---/-++ ---++/-
/+/++--/ +--/-+ ++/--/-+++/+/---+-++ /++/-
--/+++ +/+++/+
```

Her heart skips. She turns the page. More of the same. Flips through. Each page between the same as the first. She closes her eyes, hands it back to Rushin. She can hear Gardner rummaging through drawers, cursing.

"What is this?" Rushin whispers. "Is this supposed to make sense?"

Gardner comes back. "I can't find it," he says. "Maybe I left it in the bedroom." He heads that way, stops, looks from Emily to Rushin to Emily again. "What's the matter?" he says.

Emily remains silent, looks out the window.

Rushin gets up, approaches Gardner. "Nothing," he says. "It's just that this chapter's a little tough to decipher."

Gardner takes the pages from him. "You don't like it?"

Emily shakes her head, stares blankly. "I can't take this."

"What are you talking about? *What* can't you take?"

Rushin hooks his hands in his pockets, shifts from one foot to the other. "Your language is rather cryptic," he says.

"What do you mean cryptic?"

"*Look* at it!" Emily shouts. "Look at what you wrote today. Can't you see? It's all pluses and minuses and slashes. It's all *craziness. Look!*"

Gardner's eyes cloud. "What?" he says. He looks at the manuscript, turns pages. "I don't see what…" He fades off. "What?" he says, eyes darkening. The manuscript falls to the floor. Gardner clenches his fists. "No," he says. "No, please," he says. "No, they couldn't, not now, no."

Rushin puts his hand on Gardner's shoulder. "Take it easy," he says.

Gardner stares blankly. "I didn't do that," he says. He points at the scattered pages at his feet. "Did I do that?"

Rushin pats his shoulder. "It's okay, man. You're just tired, that's all. You need a breather, get your head clear."

"Pat, *no!*" Emily screams, but it's too late. Gardner swings suddenly, backhands Rushin and sends him crashing into the television stand. Emily jumps up. Gardner advances on her.

"*You!*" he says, teeth clenched. "You did it." She tries to get around him, but Gardner grabs her, throws her to the floor.

Rushin gets up, wraps his arm around Gardner's neck from behind. Gardner stomps on his foot, whirls around, punches left right left right like a powerful methodical machine. Rushin falls to his knees. Gardner grabs his hair, slams his knee into Rushin's jaw. Rushin sprawls on his back and Gardner is on him, punching, clawing, growling like a rabid dog, his face a raging mask of pain and fear.

Emily lies stunned, helplessly watching as Rushin struggles to fight back. She gets to her knees, pulls a heavy ceramic lamp from an end table.

And now Rushin's ferocity nearly matches Gardner's. He looks scared to death, spitting blood, and he squirms to his side and lashes back with an elbow to Gardner's face. Blood spurts from Gardner's nose. Rushin claws and punches, tries to throw Gardner off him, but Gardner straddles him, holds him by the ears, slams his head against the floor.

So Emily comes up behind Gardner and breaks the lamp over his head.

Gardner looks up, surprised, and Rushin reaches from the floor and flattens his knuckles on Gardner's jaw.

Gardner's eyes roll; he slumps heavily forward. Rushin heaves the body off him, rises unsteadily, gags, spits more blood.

Emily covers her face, sobs.

Rushin removes his belt, straps Gardner's hands behind his back. "Just in case," he says.

Emily phones the police, tells them to send an ambulance.

Gardner moans. Rushin sits on the floor beside him, rolls him onto his back. Blood puddles beneath his head, soaks into the carpet.

"What did we do to him?"

"Are you all right?" Emily says.

Rushin nods, jaw working.

"Are you sure? Your face looks pretty bad."

"I'm okay." He kneels over Gardner. We have to stop this bleeding. Get a towel or something."

Emily goes to the kitchen. It smells smoky. She turns on the light, and there on the table lies a half-filled plate of ashes. A sooty fork rests atop the mess. On the stove, a frying pan piled with the neat, charred ruins of burnt paper still smolders.

•

Gardner gets carried off to Bellevue strapped on a gurney, alternately struggling violently, calming down, laughing hysterically, and blubbering pitifully that he should have written a short story. This final regret remains the last coherent thought he's communicated to date. On the advice of Valerie Kopanski, Gardner is sent for treatment to the Bridgeport

Institute for Behavioral Therapy in Connecticut. Emily visits him there once a week, sits beside him in the courtyard watching him stare silently into his own personal void. What those eyes are seeing, Emily hates to imagine.

The doctors tell her that Gardner's breakdown was caused by severe bipolar disease compounded with a latent schizophrenia and obsessive fits of depression due to feelings of artistic impotence. Whatever. His resultant catatonic state—Creative Autism, they're calling it—is caused by the mind's defensive posturing in the face of unavoidable trauma. Yes, it will take time, the doctors caution, but eventually, with the administration of the proper therapeutic program, Gardner can be eased back into the real world, where he can function once again as a normal person.

Emily has her doubts. Gardner's eyes don't lie. They've left normalcy far, far behind.

Emily sees a lot of Rushin now. He's been instrumental in convincing her that Gardner's breakdown was not her fault, that there was no way she could have anticipated it. Everything happened too quickly, he tells her. Rushin's also kept her from becoming too unbearably lonely in Gardner's absence. She's even slept with him a couple of times, and though they do little more than cuddle and stroke each other, on both occasions Rushin's been patient, understanding, undemanding: in short, a true friend.

As the summer passes, Emily finds she can no longer afford to keep the apartment on 101st Street. The Science Fiction Writers of America pick up the bills for treatments Gardner's insurance doesn't cover, and the organization even sends Emily a small stipend each month "until the best young writer in the field gets back on his feet." But the rent's still too much for one person, and the memory of Gardner is tough on her there. Rushin helps her pack up and move to a cute little cubbyhole in the Bronx.

One afternoon, a week after the move, Emily busies herself unpacking the last of the boxes lining her living room wall. Rushin's due to arrive at dinnertime with Thai take-out, and she wants the place to look relatively lived in by then. Emily empties boxes of books and knickknacks, arranges them on her shelves. Tamara, the frisky Siamese kitten Rushin bought her last week to keep her company, rolls on her back, voices her sweet high-pitched mew, claws at the hem of Emily's jeans. "Go away," says Emily. "I don't have time to play."

At the bottom of the second-to-last box, Emily finds the two manila envelopes, cross-rubber-banded together, that she'd found impossible to part with after Gardner's breakdown. The first bears the still smoky-smelling remnants of Chapter One. The second holds the tattered bloodstained remnants of Chapter Two. All that remains of his novel-in-progress. She thought she'd put them out of sight and mind in the bottom drawer of Gardner's desk, but apparently, when Rushin packed up the study, he'd displayed a similar artistic aversion to disposing of something that, by some stretch of the imagination, might be considered art.

Emily hugs the package to her chest, sniffling. Oh, how fallen. That once keen mind and ambitious spirit reduced to tapping out its own demise in three symbols. She lays the manuscript aside.

In the final box she finds the preliminary sketches of her bag ladies, put away so long ago. She hasn't done a bit of work since then. She flips through the sketches, studying each closely. This is just what she needs. Inspired, she gets her paints and easel from the closet, stretches a canvas, prepares to work. She selects a sketch of a single bag lady, leaning against a storefront, staring straight at the camera. The bag lady's eyes are half-closed, lifeless. But Emily has an idea. She will give the bag lady Gardner's eyes. She will let her see what Gardner's seeing. There is a reason for the bag lady's existence, and the bag lady sees it. There is a cause for pain, suffering, degradation, death: the bag lady, through Gardner's eyes, sees it all. The bag lady will look upon infinity. Her face will glow with its terrible inevitability.

Emily sets to work.

She paints quickly, leaving the face for last, all the while picturing those eyes, Gardner's eyes, and what they must be looking upon, and what they must have seen, and beyond that to what could be seen if you had the eyes to see it.

Finally, she's ready. She begins to paint the face. The expression is right. The eyes are opening, envisioning, knowing, imagining.

The phone rings. Emily ignores it, continues painting. The phone continues ringing. Probably Rushin, calling to find out what kind of wine to bring or something. She puts down the brush, turns from the canvas and stops, suddenly disoriented. Her pulse quickens; breath comes short.

Emily has no phone. Hasn't had one connected yet.

She sways, covers her ears. Muffled ringing continues. She moves her hands from her ears to her mouth, bites her fist hard, till it hurts. The phone keeps ringing, louder than before. Tamara rubs her arched back against Emily's ankles, looks up with clear blue eyes.

"What's wrong, Emily?" Tamara says in that adorably high voice of hers. "You don't look so good."

Emily lowers her hands. "No," she says.

"You plan on answering the phone?" Tamara says. "That ringing's driving me up a wall."

Emily takes a step backward. "This isn't real. This can't be real."

"Hey, take it easy, Emily. You look beat. Why don't you take a nap or something?"

Blood thunders in Emily's skull. Her vision blurs.

"You need some rest," Tamara says. "It's that stupid bag lady you're working on. Nice idea, but the lines are all wrong. The eyes don't match the face."

Emily screams, lunges at the kitten, picks it up by its neck. "You can't talk!" she yells, tightening her grip.

"Jesus!" Tamara hisses, kicking and clawing. "Not with you choking me I can't. What are you, *crazy*?"

Emily squeezes harder. Tamara spits and snarls, rakes deep ribbons of blood in Emily's hands. Emily throws Tamara against the wall with all her strength. The kitten hits, shrieks, drops limply to the floor, head turned back over her shoulder at an awkward angle.

Emily pants, stares at the crumpled little thing.

Slowly, Tamara opens her eyes, gets to her feet, licks the fur at her shoulder, and approaches Emily archly. "Don't you know cats have nine lives?" she simpers.

Emily runs blindly to the bathroom, bolts the door behind her. A soft scratching comes from outside.

"Emily? Let me in. I was only kidding."

Emily backs away, steps into the tub, curls up, closes her eyes, covers her ears. "No, no, no," she whimpers. She can hear voices calling at her apartment door, a loud pounding. "No," she sobs. "Please, no. I don't want to be crazy. Please, please, no."

•

One hates to imagine the extent of Emily's ordeal. Just as the police prepare to break down the door, Rushin arrives with cartons of Thai food just in time to let the police in with the spare key Emily gave him. A crowd of concerned neighbors clusters in the hallway.

"Somebody killed somebody in there," says one.

"You hear the screaming?" says another. "Sounded like a baby being strangled."

Once inside, the police are unable to coax Emily out of the bathroom. They do everything they can to convince her it's safe, but she keeps babbling something about the phone ringing and the cat talking. Even Rushin can't talk her out. Finally, the police kick in the door to find Emily cowering in the bathtub, wild-eyed, bloody handed, giggling, sobbing.

They cart her off to Bellevue, and later on Rushin makes a visit to Valerie Kopanski that results in Emily being sent to the Bridgeport Institute, where a young clinical psychiatrist begins to make a name for herself in psychometric circles by publishing an article entitled "Contagious Creative Autism: Its Causes and Treatment," in which she uses Emily and Gardner as her only case studies.

But all of this comes later. First Rushin must watch them carry his one, true, heavily sedated friend out of her apartment on a stretcher; must find Tamara dead of a broken neck in the living room; must stare in puzzlement at the unfinished portrait of the bag lady with the careful calligraphies—plus, minus, and slash symbols—where her eyes should be; must pause to add things up; must convince the suspicious police that the manila-enveloped manuscript he appears to be stealing is, in fact, the beginnings of an experimental novel he's been working on that he'd asked Emily to proofread for him.

"I'm a writer," Rushin proclaims when the police open both packages and pass them around for examination. "A writer can write anything he goddamn well pleases."

Rushin must take the manuscript home with him, there to agonize, debate with his better instincts, and finally come to the conclusion that the story of the so-called Committee needs to be told. He's become convinced that the Committee really exists, in one form or another, in this dimension or that; and he's convinced that the Committee, whatever it is, has somehow touched the mind of Gardner, as well as the mind of Emily, the only woman, he's also becoming convinced, that he has ever truly loved.

And the idea that the Committee could so easily tamper with the grace, strength, and beauty of Emily's mind makes Rushin mad, yes, but it's a *calculated* kind of madness.

Yes, the story of the Committee needs to be told. He's just not convinced he possesses the writerly chops to pull it off himself. After all, he's just a second-rate minimalist in a literary era where minimalists are a dime a dozen. This is a story that demands a rampaging maximalist to tell it true.

But if Rushin's not writer enough to pull off this story, he can certainly think of a number of first-rate writers who could, and in his capacity as Chair of Columbia's Visiting Authors Reading Series, he's wined and dined a literal ton of famous writers, and it suddenly occurs to him that the perfect writer for the job, a maximalist writer of the first order, a famous writer he's had the pleasure of hosting before and becoming friendly with—that very same writer is due to visit campus next month, not to read from his work as it turns out, since he seems to be between books at present, but to give a talk on something he calls "The Venusian Threat."

Rushin decides to try to convince this writer to do the story of Emily and Gardner and the Committee justice. It's the plan of a desperate man, he realizes, and chances are very high it won't work, and if he can't convince the famous writer to take up the gauntlet, he also realizes, then the task is up to him, whether he feels capable or not. He's resigned himself to the responsibility. It's that important. Yes.

But if he does end up telling this story, he's going to tell it very carefully indeed. He's going to keep his mind safely withdrawn from the telling process. It's the *telling* that drove Gardner crazy. Imagination yields madness. Imagine something that needs to be communicated yet defies the normal media of communication, and you go crazy. You've got to be objective, ground yourself in reality. Rushin's going to *relate* a story, not *create* one.

Just the facts.

And before he begins, he'll take a few precautions.

He'll remove the plus, minus, and slash keys from his typewriter. If he needs to use one of these symbols, he'll just pencil it in. No inadvertent cryptograms in *this* story.

He'll flush the only pet he owns, a Siamese fighting fish named Sam, down the toilet. No fish talk will come bubbling to the surface to distract him.

He'll toss his phone down his apartment's trash chute. If perchance he hears it ringing, it won't be for him.

He'll give his TV, stereo, and radio to a friend. Infinity's going to have to broadcast itself directly onto his eyeballs.

If, as he's beginning to fear, his lame-brained plan to

commandeer one of America's best writers should fail, then and only then will Rushin begin writing.

·

I met the famous writer Ken Kesey at the Old King Cole Bar in the St. Regis Hotel shortly after he returned from Egypt. He was sunburnt and wind-ravaged, a wild cast to his eyes. He squinted up at the bar-length Maxfield Parrish mural in front of us as he quaffed his overpriced draft. He shook his head and snorted like a man who's seen it all—or at least the better part of it.

"You really like this place, bub?"

"I wanted to try it."

"Looks like you got what you wanted then." He pointed at King Cole sitting on his throne. "That merry old soul is grinning like he farted and blamed it on the dog."

I smiled. I was nervous. I knew he could tell. I asked about his trip.

"Oh no you don't, bub," he said, and he pulled those scorched and weather-beaten manilas from his satchel, tossed them on the bar in front of me. Suddenly the room smelled like a five-cent stogy. "Thought you could pull a fast one, huh?" He gulped his beer, coughed. "This goof's all yours."

"It's no goof. Not this."

"Bull goose goofy is what it is. Not for me. Not for anybody. I got a great notion: burn it up all over again and toss it in the Hudson to drown."

I pondered this glumly, took several sips of my club soda.

He draped a heavy arm across my back, gave my shoulder a firm squeeze. "Don't feel bad, bub. You did me a favor. I'm not about to tell *your* story, but you got me back to writing my own. Do yourself a favor. Kiss no ass. Stare mystery straight between the eyes. You'll do okay."

The famous writer Ken Kesey downed his brew and stood. "Got a bus to catch," he said.

"Don't go," I said. "Not yet."

"You're either on the bus or under it, bub." He slapped my back, turned to go.

"Wait," I said. Suddenly I couldn't bear the thought of him leaving and what that would mean to me. "You still didn't tell me about your trip."

He stopped, eyes fogging to some faraway vision. "Unbelievable," he said. "Incredible," he went on. "You can't begin to imagine the wonder and splendor of the pyramids."

"I've seen pictures," I said.

He shook his head. "Pictures are nothing. You have to *see*. I can't express the feeling—amazing, incredible."

"I can imagine," I said.

"No you can't," he said, eyes twinkling. "Imagine somebody like you imagining!"

"No," I said. "Maybe not." But then it struck me. "Yes," I said. "Yes, yes, I can."

The famous writer Ken Kesey winked at me then. "Right between the eyes," he said, and off he flew.

And I can't help myself now. A million phones ring in my ears. A billion angels dance on the keys of my typewriter. An infinite chorus of contending voices shrieks inside my skull, screaming at me that I'm tired, yes, I've been working too hard, thinking too much, I've gone too fast too far too soon past the edge and I shouldn't no, but I have, yes, but no I know maybe I should or I shouldn't or I can't when I can no but maybe no maybe I know maybe yes yes yes yes yes yes yes yes yes yes

yes yes yes yes yes yes yes yes yes yes yes yes yes yes yes yes yes
yes yes yes yes yes yes yes yes yes yes yes yes yes yes yes yes yes
yes yes yes yes yes yes yes yes yes yes yes yes yes yes yes yes yes
yes yes yes yes yes yes yes yes yes yes yes yes yes yes yes yes yes
yes yes yes yes yes yes yes yes yes yes yes yes yes yes yes yes yes
yes yes yes yes yes yes yes yes yes yes yes yes yes yes yes yes yes
yes yes yes yes yes yes yes yes yes yes yes yes yes yes yes yes yes
yes yes yes yes yes yes yes yes yes yes yes yes yes yes yes yes yes
yes yes yes yes yes yes yes yes yes yes yes yes yes yes yes yes yes
yes yes yes yes yes yes yes yes yes yes yes yes yes yes yes yes yes
yes yes yes yes yes yes yes yes yes yes yes yes yes yes yes yes yes
yes yes yes yes yes yes yes yes yes yes yes yes yes yes yes yes yes
yes yes yes yes yes yes yes yes yes yes yes yes yes yes yes yes yes
yes yes yes yes yes yes yes yes yes yes yes yes yes yes yes yes yes
yes yes yes yes yes yes yes yes yes yes yes yes yes yes yes yes yes
yes yes yes yes yes yes yes yes yes yes yes yes yes yes yes yes yes
yes yes yes yes yes yes yes yes yes yes yes yes yes yes yes yes yes
yes yes yes yes yes yes yes yes yes yes yes yes yes yes yes yes yes
yes yes yes yes yes yes yes yes yes yes yes yes yes yes yes yes yes
yes yes yes yes yes yes yes yes yes yes yes yes yes yes yes yes yes
yes yes yes yes yes yes yes yes yes yes yes yes yes yes yes yes yes
yes yes yes yes yes yes yes yes yes yes yes yes yes yes yes yes yes
yes yes yes yes yes yes yes yes yes yes yes yes yes yes yes yes yes
yes yes yes yes yes yes yes yes yes yes yes yes yes yes yes yes yes
yes yes yes yes yes yes yes yes yes yes yes yes yes yes yes yes yes
yes yes yes yes yes yes yes yes yes yes yes yes yes yes yes yes yes
yes yes yes yes yes yes yes yes yes yes yes yes yes yes yes yes yes
yes yes yes yes yes yes yes yes yes yes yes yes yes yes yes yes yes
yes yes yes yes yes yes yes yes yes yes yes yes yes yes yes yes yes
yes yes yes yes yes yes yes yes yes yes yes yes yes yes yes yes yes
yes yes yes yes yes yes yes yes yes yes yes yes yes yes yes yes yes
yes yes yes yes yes yes yes yes yes yes yes yes yes yes yes yes yes

yes yes yes yes yes yes yes yes yes yes yes yes yes yes yes yes
yes yes yes yes yes yes yes yes yes yes yes yes yes yes yes yes
yes yes yes yes yes yes yes yes yes yes yes yes yes yes yes yes
yes yes yes yes yes yes yes yes yes yes yes yes yes yes yes yes
yes yes yes yes yes yes yes yes yes yes yes yes yes yes yes yes
yes yes yes yes yes yes yes yes yes yes yes yes yes yes yes yes
yes yes yes yes yes yes yes yes yes yes yes yes yes yes yes yes

yes yes yes yes yes yes yes   yes yes yes yes yes yes yes
yes yes yes yes yes yes yes   yes yes yes yes yes yes yes
yes yes yes yes yes yes yes   yes yes yes yes yes yes yes
yes yes yes yes yes yes yes   yes yes yes yes yes yes yes
yes yes yes yes yes yes yes   yes yes yes yes yes yes yes
yes yes yes yes yes yes yes   yes yes yes yes yes yes yes
yes yes   yes yes
yes yes   yes yes
yes yes yes yes yes yes yes   yes yes yes yes yes yes yes
yes yes yes yes yes yes yes   yes yes yes yes yes yes yes
yes yes yes yes yes yes yes   yes yes yes yes yes yes yes
yes yes yes yes yes yes yes   yes yes yes yes yes yes yes
yes yes yes yes yes yes yes   yes yes yes yes yes yes yes
yes yes yes yes yes yes yes   yes yes yes yes yes yes yes

yes yes yes yes yes yes yes yes yes yes yes yes yes yes yes yes
yes yes yes yes yes yes yes yes yes yes yes yes yes yes yes yes
yes yes yes yes yes yes yes yes yes yes yes yes yes yes yes yes
yes yes yes yes yes yes yes yes yes yes yes yes yes yes yes yes
yes yes yes yes yes yes yes yes yes yes yes yes yes yes yes yes
yes yes yes yes yes yes yes yes yes yes yes yes yes yes yes yes
yes yes yes yes yes yes yes yes yes yes yes yes yes yes yes yes
yes yes yes yes yes yes yes yes yes yes yes yes yes yes yes yes
yes yes yes yes yes yes yes yes yes yes yes yes yes yes yes yes
yes yes yes yes yes yes yes yes yes yes yes yes yes yes yes yes

yes yes yes yes yes yes yes yes yes yes yes yes yes yes yes yes yes
yes yes yes yes yes yes yes yes yes yes yes yes yes yes yes yes yes
yes yes yes yes yes yes yes yes yes yes yes yes yes yes yes yes y
yes yes yes yes yes yes yes yes yes yes yes yes yes yes yes yes yes
yes yes yes yes yes yes yes yes yes yes yes yes yes yes yes yes yes
yes yes yes yes yes yes yes yes yes yes yes yes yes yes yes yes yes
yes yes yes yes yes yes yes yes yes yes yes yes yes yes yes yes yes
yes yes yes yes yes yes yes yes yes yes yes yes yes yes yes yes yes
yes yes yes yes yes yes yes yes yes yes yes yes yes yes yes yes yes
yes yes yes yes yes yes yes yes yes yes yes yes yes yes yes yes yes
yes yes yes yes yes yes yes yes yes yes yes yes yes yes yes yes yes
yes yes yes yes yes yes yes yes yes yes yes yes yes yes yes yes yes
yes yes yes yes yes yes yes yes yes yes yes yes yes yes yes yes yes
yes yes   yes yes

yes yes   yes yes

yes yes yes yes yes yes yes yes yes yes yes yes yes yes yes yes yes
yes yes yes yes yes yes yes yes yes yes yes yes yes yes yes yes yes
yes yes yes yes yes yes yes yes yes yes yes yes yes yes yes yes yes
yes yes yes yes yes yes yes yes yes yes yes yes yes yes yes yes yes
yes yes yes yes yes yes yes yes yes yes yes yes yes yes yes yes yes
yes yes yes yes yes yes yes yes yes yes yes yes yes yes yes yes yes
yes yes yes yes yes yes yes yes yes yes yes yes yes yes yes yes yes
yes yes yes yes yes yes yes yes yes yes yes yes yes yes yes yes yes
yes yes yes yes yes yes yes yes yes yes yes yes yes yes yes yes yes
yes yes yes yes yes yes yes yes yes yes yes yes yes yes yes yes yes
yes yes yes yes yes yes yes yes yes yes yes yes yes yes yes yes yes
yes yes yes yes yes yes yes yes yes yes yes yes yes yes yes yes yes
yes yes yes yes yes yes yes yes yes yes yes yes yes yes yes yes yes
yes yes yes yes yes yes yes yes yes yes yes yes yes yes yes yes yes
yes yes yes yes yes yes yes yes yes yes yes yes yes yes yes yes yes
yes yes yes yes yes yes yes yes yes yes yes yes yes yes yes yes yes

yes yes yes yes yes yes yes yes yes yes yes yes yes yes yes yes
yes yes yes yes yes yes yes yes yes yes yes yes yes yes yes yes
yes yes yes yes yes yes yes yes yes yes yes yes yes yes yes yes
yes yes yes yes yes yes yes yes yes yes yes yes yes yes yes yes
yes yes yes yes yes yes yes yes yes yes yes yes yes yes yes yes
yes yes yes yes yes yes yes yes yes yes yes yes yes yes yes yes
yes yes yes yes yes yes yes yes yes yes yes yes yes yes yes yes
yes yes yes yes yes yes yes yes yes yes yes yes yes yes yes yes
yes yes yes yes yes yes yes yes yes yes yes yes yes yes yes yes
yes yes yes yes yes yes yes yes yes yes yes yes yes yes yes yes
yes yes yes yes yes yes yes yes yes yes yes   yes yes yes
yes yes yes yes yes yes yes yes yes yes yes   yes yes yes yes
yes yes yes yes yes yes yes yes yes yes   yes yes yes yes yes
yes yes yes yes yes yes yes yes yes   yes yes yes yes yes yes
yes yes yes yes yes yes yes yes   yes yes yes yes yes yes yes
yes yes yes yes yes yes yes   yes yes yes yes yes yes yes yes
yes yes yes yes yes yes   yes yes yes yes yes yes yes yes yes
yes yes yes yes yes   yes yes yes yes yes yes yes yes yes yes
yes yes yes yes   yes yes yes yes yes yes yes yes yes yes yes
yes yes yes   yes yes yes yes yes yes yes yes yes yes yes
yes yes yes yes yes yes yes yes yes yes yes yes yes yes yes yes
yes yes yes yes yes yes yes yes yes yes yes yes yes yes yes yes
yes yes yes yes yes yes yes yes yes yes yes yes yes yes yes yes
yes yes yes yes yes yes yes yes yes yes yes yes yes yes yes yes
yes yes yes yes yes yes yes yes yes yes yes yes yes yes yes yes
yes yes yes yes yes yes yes yes yes yes yes yes yes yes yes yes
yes yes yes yes yes yes yes yes yes yes yes yes yes yes yes yes
yes yes yes yes yes yes yes yes yes yes yes yes yes yes yes yes
yes yes yes yes yes yes yes yes yes yes yes yes yes yes yes yes
yes yes yes yes yes yes yes yes yes yes yes yes yes yes yes yes
yes yes yes yes yes yes yes yes yes yes yes yes yes yes yes yes
yes yes yes yes yes yes yes yes yes yes yes yes yes yes yes yes

MORE FROM BURROW PRESS

The Call: a virtual parable
by Pat Rushin
978-1-941681-90-9

"Pat Rushin is out of his fucking mind. I like that in a writer; that and his daredevil usage of the semi-colon and asterisk make *The Call* unputdownable."
–Terry Gilliam, director of *The Zero Theorem*

Pinkies: stories
by Shane Hinton
978-1-941681-92-3

"If Kafka got it on with Flannery O' Connor, *Pinkies* would be their love child."
– Lidia Yuknavitch, *The Small Backs of Children*

Songs for the Deaf: stories
by John Henry Fleming
978-0-9849538-5-1

"*Songs for the Deaf* is a joyful, deranged, endlessly surprising book. Fleming's prose is glorious music; his rhythms will get into your bloodstream, and his images will sink into your dreams."
– Karen Russell, *Swamplandia!*

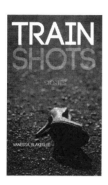

Train Shots: stories
by Vanessa Blakeslee
978-0-9849538-4-4

"*Train Shots* is more than a promising first collection by a formidably talented writer; it is a haunting story collection of the first order."
– John Dufresne, *No Regrets, Coyote*

15 Views of Miami
edited by Jaquira Díaz
978-0-9849538-3-7

Named one of the 7 best books about Miami by the *Miami New Times*

Forty Martyrs
by Philip F. Deaver
978-1-941681-94-7

"I could hardly stop reading, from first to last."
– Ann Beattie, *The State We're In*

SUBSCRIBE TO BURROW PRESS 2017

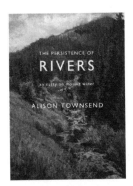

The Persistence of Rivers
by Alison Townsend
978-1-941681-83-1

"Townsend's articulation of sorrow has always cast an aura of beauty and deepest, truest instruction."
– Sharon Doubiago, *My Father's Love*

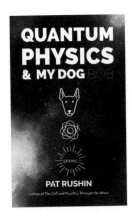

Quantum Physics & My Dog Bob
by Pat Rushin
978-1-941681-81-7

"The stories in Quantum Physics & My Dog Bob are brilliant and funny. Dark funny. These stories will easily change the way you observe the world."
— Virgil Suarez, *The Soviet Circus Comes to Havana*

BURROWPRESS.COM/SUBSCRIBE

We Can't Help it if We're From Florida
edited by Shane Hinton
978-1-941681-87-9

"While no book could ever fully explain the mysteries of today's Sunshine State, this smart chorus of varied and brilliant voices comes as close as any I've read."
— Lauren Groff, *Fates & Furies*

Other Orlandos
edited by Leslie Salas

ORLANDO is a fern awaiting a patent, an obscure car model, Virginia Woolf's creation, a power plant in Johannesburg, an epic poem, an opera, a celebrity mask / marital aid... In this anthology of fiction, nonfiction & poetry, Orlando is anything but the city so often associated with theme parks.

Burrow Press is a 501(c)(3) nonprofit literary publisher based in Orlando, FL. The Illiterati is Burrow Press' sorta-secretive community of book-loving weirdos. Membership in the illiterati supports our mission of publishing a lasting body of literature (with a focus on Florida), and fostering literary community in Orlando. Through our print books, online journal, reading series and radio show, BP has served over 800 writers since its founding in 2010.

ILLITERATI MEMBERSHIP LEVELS

$60 SUBSCRIBER

Name recognition in a year's worth of BP books
4-book BP subscription package
& ebooks, free shipping

$40 LOCAL

Name recognition in a year's worth of BP books
Priority seating for a year of Functionally Literate events
Commemorative Functionally Literate koozie

$20 TOURIST

Tote bag designed by Boy Kong

$120 ORLANDOAN

All of the above perks.

Join the Illiterati: burrowpress.com/hush

General donations: burrowpress.com/donate